Tales of the A.E.G.I.S. Space Rangers

Renegades of Mars

By Todd Downing

FIRST EDITION

ISBN: 978-1-961545-12-0
Copyright © 2025 Todd Downing & Deep7 Press
All Rights Reserved Worldwide
Edited by Raechelle Downing & Randy Hensel
Cover design by Todd Downing

WWW.TODDDOWNING.COM

Deep7 Press is a subsidiary of Despot Media, LLC
1214 Woods Rd SE Port Orchard, WA 98366 USA
WWW.DEEP7.COM

In salute to the late, great Alex Raymond

Foreword

Apologies for the delay.

I know fans of the *Airship Daedalus* setting have been waiting ever so patiently for these next stories, and it's taken a minute to get the work to a point where I was actually satisfied with the end product.

1930s pulp adventure in the raypunk milieu isn't currently the most popular or salable genre to write, and with the exception of Dr. Nariaal, I had a completely new cast of characters to get to know. There was a considerable amount of character psychoanalysis and wheel reinvention, to be sure.

I had to find my heroine and give her Important Things to Do, including walking a tightrope between serving the colonial interest and advocating for her people.

And punching Nazis. That pretty much goes without saying. My pulp characters will always punch Nazis. Repeatedly and unapologetically.

The heroes of the *Airship Daedalus* novels (and radio episodes, and roleplaying game, and comics) punched their Nazi-equivalents in the form of an occult fascist army, which worked fine for a setting in the interbellum 1920s. But by the time we push into the 1930s and the space race made possible by reverse-engineered Martian war machines, we're really dealing with the run-up to World War Two, and that means honest to gawd Nazis.

Rest assured, including one of the worst fascist movements to ever exist on Earth as a collective villain is not something I take lightly. They were truly horrible—this is historical fact and not in any way debatable—and executed multiple crimes against humanity before the rest of the world said *"hell no"* and ushered them into oblivion. When a group exploits collective tolerance to grab power and normalize genocide, I reckon they've broken the social contract, and don't get to sit at the adult table ever again.

But every few generations, when the worst people insist on giving past monsters an image rehab, I feel it's important to trot out some goose-stepping, Roman-saluting baddies for the good guys to mow down—if only as a reminder that *fascists get nothing*.

So I had to put in the research and the actual writing, in between a few adventure game titles on the slate and multiple deaths in the family.

Some days I just didn't have the gumption.

The good news is that it's finished, and you're reading it now. Like the *Airship Daedalus* series and *AEGIS Tales* anthologies, this is what I call "kitchen sink pulp". In other words, it has a bit of every pulp genre you might care to find: from science fiction (obviously) to western, to a little romance and a hint of horror, and a healthy dose of two-fisted adventure.

For clarity's sake, this story takes place in the same *Airship Daedalus/AEGIS Tales* universe (known as the AEGISverse), a few short years after *Raiders of the Red Storm*—just on a different planet. You don't have to have read the *Airship Daedalus* series before diving into this book, but it helps set the stage. Your call, of course.

Although the process took its sweet time, I feel like I truly got to know my heroine and her team, and now they're clamoring around in my head with more stories to tell. Who knows? If you tell your friends and get them to buy a copy, I might even be able to write the next one.

Please enjoy the next phase of the AEGIS-verse.

- Todd Downing, Port Orchard, WA
  Summer, 2025

Acknowledgments

I must salute the giants upon whose shoulders I stand in the telling of this story: Alex Raymond, Ray Bradbury, Edgar Rice Burroughs, and H.G. Wells—the latter two for certain names and story elements in the public domain. The story is mine—I've simply borrowed some of their toys for my sandbox.

Many thanks to the *Airship Daedalus* fan community, to lovers of raypunk and retro-futurism in general, and to my fellow authors in our group Discord: John Sullivan (AKA Mark Parragh, AKA E.J. Blaine), Martin Shannon, Trish Heinrich, and Andrew Marnik.

To my lovely and talented wife Raechelle, thanks for giving this book your attention in the midst of a full slate of authors you edit for. Likewise, thanks to Randy Hensel for your multiple eyes on this work (hey, two qualifies as "multiple").

CONTENT WARNING: substance use/abuse, loss of agency, references to slavery & human trafficking, science fiction violence, death, quasi-occult & supernatural themes.

CHAPTER 1

Carter Flats, Mars, 1936

*M*ining towns are all the same, Sinari thought.

There were only two main streets, running east-west and north-south, effectively breaking the settlement into quarters. At one end, The Docks featured a landing pad large enough to accommodate cargo haulers, with storage warehouses and an office center. Opposite the The Docks were The Squats, an array of concrete dwellings and scrap metal shanties where the local workers lived. There was also a granary, a communal well pump house, and the water storage tanks.

The Brass was what locals called the administrative sector of town. It contained a power station and solar array, with a few scattered offices. The marshal's office, which included a modest jail, faced outward into the main intersection, allowing for easy access anywhere in the settlement.

The final quarter went by many names depending on the locale, but generally included at least one bar—with or without gambling and more "personal services"—plus a mercantile area of hardware stores, food vendors, and mechanical service shops. Here, it was known simply as The Market.

Surrounding the town was a four-meter-high concrete wall, protecting those within against the blistering sandstorms that plagued the northern hemisphere.

Despite Terrans having only arrived a year ago, the planet was dotted with countless such settlements. Carter Flats was perhaps the most quintessential of them all, and yet it had the distinction of being built among the ruins of a much older civilization in the shadow of Uranius Patera. It also had the benefit of being less than a hundred kilometers from the Allied Space Administration's spaceport, which carried the uniquely poetic designation of MARS 1.

At midday, Carter Flats was largely quiet, devoid of most foot and vehicle traffic. Not unusual, seeing as how most residents were away at the mines, hacking at rich veins of thermacite crystal underground. That left service industry people, merchants, and criminals.

Sinari Vohn was looking for the latter.

She pulled the hood on her poncho a bit lower, violet eyes piercing the unusually still afternoon with a single-minded intensity. The woman was tall and athletically built, clad in a "townie" wardrobe consisting of a linen shirt, leggings of gray denim, and brown leather work boots. The belt encircling her waist held sundry tools and gadgets, and perhaps a weapon—maybe two. Fortunately the hooded poncho kept such things hidden from public notice as she strode across the main thoroughfare toward the bar where her fence was waiting.

Neon script on the windowless exterior wall blinked *ZOLA'S* in vibrant green. The place had recently returned to indigenous ownership when the last proprietor was shot dead behind the bar. It wasn't like he didn't have it coming. Honestly, you don't start a tavern on Mars and call it *BAR SOOM*. Not if you're human. The native population hadn't found it clever, to say the least. Given that *Barsoom* was the planet's indigenous name, a sacred name, the outcome was probably not a terrible shock.

Like most commercial structures in the settlement, the bar was made of concrete and corrugated steel, with a rounded roof that repelled the elements—the primary element being wind, and whatever the wind might be carrying at any given time. It was also built half underground, requiring patrons to descend a short flight of stairs to the door.

Sinari entered slowly, letting her eyes adjust to the dim interior. There was just enough space to accommodate six tables and a bar without stools, and a small storage room off the back. The walls were covered in tin signs advertising popular brands like Whistle soda and Jax beer.

A human couple in work clothes stood at the bar. The woman perused song selections on the Wurlitzer automatic phonograph as the strains of *Red Sails in the Sunset* by Guy Lombardo and His Orchestra filled the air.

Three more men were having an animated discussion about mobile mining drills at the table nearest the door. Two others leaned against one wall, deep in quiet conversation, a boot apiece resting on the bench beneath them.

At the farthest table sat a solitary man in a dusty gray driving cap and dark overcoat. He looked simultaneously like he absolutely belonged there, and yet completely out of place.

The immediate area behind the bar was occupied by Zola. Vaguely humanoid, she stood over two and a half meters tall, with dusky green skin and bug-like eyes. A second pair of arms sprouting halfway down her ribcage made tending bar a breeze; two could be filling an order from the tap while the other two washed and dried the dirty glasses. Her venerable age was belied by a boisterous, lively attitude and manual dexterity that would have impressed any master of the shell game.

Sinari took a step into the tavern and lowered her hood, revealing a copper-red complexion and raven black hair pulled back in a ponytail. A few of the human patrons threw her glances that ranged from approving to downright salacious, but she ignored the attention, silently appraising each of the scruffy half-drunk men and knowing none of them would be a problem. The scathing look from the woman standing by the bar read more competitive than lustful, as she slid closer to her man. She'd probably heard—and believed—rumors of Red Martian allure, a combination of pheromones and sexual appetite. Such rumors were not surprising. After all, one of the main tools of oppression by a conquering society is the exotification of native people.

Sinari figured the man sitting alone in the back was her guy, and his nod confirmed her assumption. She made her way to his table, pausing at the bar for a shot of Martian whiskey, which she threw back like a pro. The lone man watched her every move, his eyes following as she tossed a coin on the bar and came to sit across from him.

Regarding him briefly, she made a mental record of his features: he was tall, slender and sinewy, with intense eyes and a mouth that was little more than a lipless line.

"You Karpis?" she asked, settling onto the stool across from him.

The man's eyes darted from side to side. "Ray," he grunted.

"I hear you're looking to move some thermacite."

"Yeah," he reached below the table, producing a small leather pouch and placing it on the table. "Here's a sample."

Sinari threw a brief glance over her shoulder at the bar. The couple was now chatting with Zola about Martian cuisine. No one was paying her or the fence any notice. Quietly, she pulled open the pouch and emptied its contents onto the table. A single ruby-colored crystal about the size of her index finger sparkled in the modest light from the bar. She would need to check it with a loupe, but at first glance it sure looked like the real deal.

"Where did you get it?"

The fence shifted on his stool. "Not that it's any of your business—it was skimmed from a mining operation out in Tempe Terra."

Sinari did some quick calculations in her head. She didn't know of any crystal mining in Tempe Terra, a vast desert plain scarred with deep canyons about two hundred kilometers to the northeast. Nor had she heard of any of the more local operations being skimmed. Ultimately, he was probably lying to protect his true source, so it didn't really matter.

"How much do you need to move?" she wondered, putting the crystal back into the pouch.

Ray's eyes shifted once again, nonexistent lips peeling back over yellow teeth in a sneer as he leaned forward. "Two hundred shards, just like that one. But I can probably get more."

Before she could ask their location, she heard the rhythmic tap of a boot against a metal case beneath the table. She frowned, finding his smile inherently creepy.

"All shards?" Sinari asked, eyes the color of amethyst probing for clues in the man's body language. "Nothing larger?"

If he'd been nervous before, Ray was ratcheting toward full-blown paranoia. "Nothing larger? What, are you trying to power guns for a fleet of rockets? These shards are good to go as-is. Ten Gs and the case is yours."

Sinari leaned back, assessing the man and his increasingly erratic demeanor. The fingers of his left hand drummed the table, and he was beginning to sweat. "I can do five," she countered.

Ray's eyes darted from the bar to the door. He looked like he was counting paces. "Come on, doll. Make it worth my while. How 'bout nine?"

"That's almost retail value, Ray."

"Yeah, but where you gonna get two hundred shards in one go, and rifle-ready to boot?"

Sighing, she appeared to acquiesce. "I can go as high as seven."

"Done," Ray snapped, wiping the sweat from his brow with his left hand, his right still hidden below the table.

Sinari lifted a roll of cash from within her poncho, placing it on the table. "Seven thousand U.S. dollars."

Ray looked at the cash and fresh sweat beaded on the bridge of his nose. "What the hell?" he hissed, trying not to draw attention.

"Who said cash? I need ingots, sister. I need payment in gold."

Cocking her head inquisitively, Sinari tried to anticipate what his next move might be. "Ray... Ray... buddy," she cooed softly, trying to ease him off the ledge. "I can't just lug around six kilos of gold ingots on my person." She patted the roll of bills on the table with a fingerless glove. "Greenbacks spend just fine. But if you still want gold, you can buy it at the spaceport."

He took a frustrated breath and blinked hard. "A-a-alright," he stammered, shooting glances past her shoulder toward the door. "Alright. I'll take the cash."

Sinari knew that his right hand, still hidden beneath the table for the past few minutes, would either produce the case containing the stolen thermacite or a weapon. Given his demeanor, it was even money which. As much as she hoped he wouldn't be stupid enough to start a brawl, she could smell his nervous desperation, and therefore couldn't rule it out.

"Here's your crystal," he growled as he swung the metal case at her head.

Sinari leaned back on the stool, and the case narrowly missed her jaw. Gripping Ray's left hand as it snatched the roll of currency, she pulled him toward her and shoved the center pedestal of the table with a hard kick, knocking him off balance. He sailed over her, upending another table and scrambling upright about ten paces nearer the door.

As the other patrons turned, trying to register what had just happened, the fence leaped to his feet. Still holding the metal case in his right hand, he stuffed the cash roll into his belt with his left, cross-drawing a Colt automatic in one fluid motion.

Zola froze in place, but a pint glass fell from her grip and shattered on the concrete floor.

"Don't nobody move," Ray warned the occupants of the bar. Noticing Sinari's slow reach behind her back, he flicked the hammer back on his pistol, brandishing it in her direction. "...or try anything funny."

Sinari showed her hands. "Why the double-cross, Ray?" she prodded.

"'Cause somethin' don't smell right. And when it don't smell right, I hit the road, see?" He took a small step backward, toward the door. "Sorry it didn't work out, doll. Consider the cash as payment for my time."

Ray Karpis tracked the pistol across the room once more, backing toward the exit. As he reached the bottom of the stairwell to the outside world, his gaze shifted momentarily toward the trio near the door—long enough for Sinari to draw her own sidearm.

A beam of brilliant red light erupted from the chrome ray gun along with a sound like a piece of metal being scraped down a high-tension cable. She'd unfortunately fired on a quick-draw from a crouch, and her shot went wide by several inches, leaving a charred one-inch pockmark in the concrete wall.

Patrons immediately dived behind tables as Karpis scrambled away up the stairs to the open streets of Carter Flats. Sinari bolted after him, casting a hasty, "Sorry about the mess, Zola!" over her shoulder.

Karpis squinted as his eyes were overcome by the bleak, bright Martian afternoon. Clearing the top step onto street level, he turned and backed away from the bar, keeping his pistol trained on the exit.

There was a muffled thump, and he fell unconscious to the dusty ground.

Marshal Henry Hu lowered the shoulder stock of the shotgun in his hands. "Well, well," he mused. "Creepy Karpis. What's your ugly mug doing in my town?"

The lawman was of average height and broad-chested, with a complexion like day-old coffee and a jaw like an iron trap. He wore dungarees and cowboy boots, with the sleeves of a pale green work shirt peeking out from a brown leather vest. His head was shaved under the Stetson hat which sat cocked at an angle, and a black mustache traced a broad upper lip. His eyes had what Sinari understood to be a typically Asian shape, and they scanned the bar exterior as Sinari poked her head out. When she saw the coast was clear, she went to greet the marshal as he cuffed the unconscious fence—hands front—in a pair of iron shackles.

"Howdy," she offered. "Thanks for the save." She liked the marshal. He was stalwart and kind—to her, anyway. He seemed to care about the plight of native Martians trying to survive in the land rush and industrial onslaught the Treaties had ushered in, though he would never admit it out loud. *Folks are folks,* he'd say. *Red or Green, brown or white. Good folks take care of other good folks. Bad folks are MY job.*

The look he gave was one of tired recognition. "Don't thank me yet," he said. "You're coming back to my office to answer some questions."

Sinari Vohn took a breath and let it out in an audible sigh. "Of course," she nodded.

"This yours?" the marshal asked, handing her the roll of cash next to the captured thug.

She nodded again, accepting the money as she holstered the ray gun under her poncho and watched him finish searching the man.

The marshal picked up the discarded Colt and pulled the clip free. Racking the slide to eject the chambered cartridge, he slipped the gun, magazine, and .45 caliber round into his belt. Then he grabbed Karpis by the back of his jacket collar and began to drag the gangster on his backside, still clutching the shotgun in one hand. He nodded at the metal case lying in the street, indicating for Sinari to follow.

"Grab that, will ya?"

The marshal's office was just across the road, opposite Zola's on the front-facing corner of The Brass. Sinari held the door open for Hu as he entered and proceeded directly to a vacant jail cell, rolling Karpis onto the cot within. Releasing the man's shackled wrists, he slammed the bars shut and locked the door.

"Am I mistaken," Sinari began, "or did I see a look of recognition on your face when I came out of Zola's? Just who is that guy?"

"Take a look on my wall," said the marshal, gesturing at an array of wanted posters pinned to a massive cork board opposite the single desk occupying the center of the room.

"Alvin Francis Karpa... Karpavick... vick-
-ee-us," she squinted at the text on the poster,
having some trouble with the Lithuanian sur-
name.

The marshal rounded the desk to plop
down in a wooden rolling chair. "Yeah, I can't
pronounce it either. He goes by Alvin Karpis,
prefers Ray, but those who know him best actually call him Creepy." Pondering the
mugshot on the FBI flyer, he noted the dour
expression and intense gaze. "He's supposed
to be running with the Barker-Karpis Gang
back in the States. Last of the FBI's Most
Wanted who's still alive."

"So, what's he doing on Mars?" Sinari
asked, flipping open the metal case full of
sparkling blood-red crystal shards. "And why
is he selling black market thermacite?"

Henry Hu peered into the case and sighed,
resigned. "You know as much about that as I
do."

AEGIS wasn't paying him enough for this
gig.

CHAPTER 2

Sinari revved the throttle on the custom Triumph motorcycle, a steady crossbreeze whipping high desert sand across her goggles. Her hooded poncho and cowl kept the lion's share from tearing at her flesh, but she knew she'd be washing it out of the most unlikely nooks and crannies in her sleeping quarters later that night. The afternoon sun hung low in the sky over Amazonis Planitia, and the Triumph's rubber tires hummed along the outstretched road across a vast pale orange expanse.

At just 26, Sinari was too young to remember the once verdant northern plains, covered in lush forests and criss-crossed by mighty rivers. By the time she'd hatched from the sole surviving egg in her mother's clutch, Martian society—and the very biosphere itself—was on the verge of collapsing.

For generations, the air they breathed had been supplemented by enormous atmospheric processors constructed at set points around the globe. Ancient technology put in place by a mysterious race known simply as the Elders. In the indigenous oral tradition, the Elder Martians were said to have arrived from another place, possibly some eldritch dimension. Here, and elsewhere in the solar system, they selectively bred humanoid life. For what purpose was unknown, although both legend and recent evidence supported the theory that such humanoid life was intended to be a food source.

In the year Terrans designated 1894, one of the mammoth air processors malfunctioned, and the local nest of Elder Martians awoke from centuries of slumber, each one a writhing, tentacled horror three meters tall and ravenous for humanoid blood. Their towering tripod war machines rained terror on the local population, and when the dust settled, the Elders realized that, with their stasis cycle interrupted, they would not be able to return underground.

Instead, they set their sights on an island in the Atlantic Ocean on Earth, which was then at close opposition. Even without a full invasion force, the Elder Martians forecast an easy victory, as they had the superior technology and could harvest their human food at will. There were two factors they hadn't considered, and had no way of predicting: the dogged resilience of the British populace, and the highly successful viruses which had evolved alongside humankind.

In a short time, the Martian invaders were dead from infection, and their alien technology was in the hands of the British government. The invasion was a national secret kept for over thirty years while their most brilliant minds studied and reverse-engineered the salvaged war machines. By 1930, they'd learned the Elder Martian secret of using special crystals to amplify electrical or kinetic charge focused through them. In 1932, the British government, along with the United States and the financial consortium behind the Allied Enterprise Group for International Security, developed the first wave of manned space rocketry. And from there, interplanetary exploration occurred at lightning speed.

By 1934, the Allied Space Administration or ASA had been formed, lunar colonization was underway, and contact was made with multiple humanoid species living in a hollow biosphere underground. That same year, military-backed mercantile expeditions formalized treaties with various city-states on Venus.

Then, in 1935, the first Terran expeditions arrived on Mars. What the human explorers found was a population devastated by decades of internal warfare and disease, on the precipice of complete environmental collapse. In the guise of saviors, Terrans swooped in, repaired the atmospheric processors, and began the work of conquering an already conquered people through bureaucracy and economy. With nary a shot fired, Mars became a vassal state of the United Kingdom, the United States, and their allies. The ASA governed the day-to-day operations of interplanetary travel and trade, while AEGIS enforced the rule of law.

While Sinari had grown up during the worst of Martian decline, it was disheartening nonetheless to watch as her people became second-class citizens, coerced into mining crystal for slave wages, working as muscle for one of the many Terran criminal syndicates, or trafficked into the sex trade.

And yet it was far better than what the Nazis offered.

The first of the Waffen-SS had arrived only eight months ago, and their numbers were on the rise. At first, they stuck to remote outposts, pressing the local tribes into service, mostly to provide physical labor for their own mining operations. But more recently they'd begun to show up in Allied company towns and spaceports, spreading fascist propaganda and sowing discontent. Their spies were everywhere.

The rise of Uranius Patera hove into view on the horizon, and Sinari revved the throttle again, increasing speed. The Triumph Silent Scout was of British manufacture, its original single-cylinder engine replaced by twin electric generators, making the vehicle much more accurately named. A battery was hidden within the chrome teardrop gas tank, and dual Edison-DiMarco dynamos thrummed within their housing under the saddle, sending the cycle onward, toward ASA Mars 1.

The spaceport was the epitome of "Jazz Moderne", functional design with a streamlined aesthetic. Administrative buildings with colossal window panels surrounded a bustling city center. Landing pads, docking bays, and hangar facilities fanned out to the west.

She passed through a business district of unfinished skyscrapers that reached spiky fingers of steel toward the sky, realizing she hadn't noticed the transition from packed desert soil to concrete beneath her wheels. Winding her way across the city center, she passed block after block of retail shops, restaurants, and bars. The sun was already falling below the shadow of the city skyline, streetlights and neon signs flickering on like a million candles.

On her left was a street which led through "Red Harlem", a vibrant neighborhood full of nightclubs and theaters, where one could hear the lively strains of jazz music pouring out of a given establishment at any time of day or night. American settlers from Earth had brought the musical form with them, and Red Martians embraced it with gusto. They were mad for anything jazz and jazz-related, from the music itself to the art and fashion, to the associated vices.

Sinari loved escaping into the intricate compositions, and often whiled away evenings in the smoky bars on the strip, thrilling to live bands and dancing. And perhaps a hazy night with some Terran hash and a stranger's bed. It was a way to escape the daily realities of being a powerless serf in her own land.

Of course, the latter activities were becoming more scarce, as she found recovery took longer the older she got. Regardless, she was still on the clock, and had to file her report of the day's business. Red Harlem would have to wait.

Arriving at last in the western quarter, Sinari could see the Allied Space Administration building, its proud edifice of sweeping chrome and banks of windows, with a wide concrete staircase ascending from the street to a set of oversize entry doors. It reminded her of the film *Metropolis*, when the power station transitioned to the face of Moloch, swallowing the hapless workers into a ravenous maw. Movies were another popular Earth export, wowing the indigenous Martians, who had their own strong storytelling tradition.

Angling the Triumph to make a right turn, she circled to the back of the block, to a parking bay reserved for ASA and AEGIS personnel. A shimmering blue Lenzium field prevented unauthorized passage, which Sinari bypassed at a security pylon by inputting a numeric code on a rotary dial.

She quickly found a stall, parked and dismounted, raising the driving goggles to rest on her forehead. Coated in road dust and back aching from the ride, Sinari made her way into the open lobby. The newly-constructed facility was bathed in natural light through endless rows of tempered glass panels. A translucent causeway provided access from the docking bays outside to the bureaucracy within. The ASA furnished official, government-sanctioned transport from Earth to Luna, Mars, and Venus, as well as the infrastructure on the ground. Customs, commercial import-export and warehouse facilities, and offices for various embassies and government authorities resided here, with leased offices and retail shops on the ground floor surrounding an expansive common space.

Sinari stepped onto a chrome escalator and rode to the third floor, across the open terrace into the dimly-lit Mars headquarters of the Allied Enterprise Group for Interplanetary Security. Launched by a consortium of American industrialists in the mid-'20s, the AEGIS acronym had originally stood for American Enterprise Group for International Security, but in the ensuing decade, as more nations had joined in the effort, and as humankind's reach now stretched to the inner solar system, its meaning—though not its mission—had changed.

On Earth, AEGIS had been responsible for keeping the creeping menace of occult organizations like the *Astrum Argentum* at bay. People such as "Captain Stratosphere" Jack McGraw, Dorothy "Doc" Starr, and Joe "Seer" Desmond had become world-renowned for their role in saving the planet from all manner of eldritch terrors. Now, with an interplanetary crystal boom in full swing, AEGIS had been tasked with maintaining law and order on the new frontier.

Sinari entered the office, recalling the day the ASA made contact. Her clan was starving. Martian scientists had estimated perhaps six months to a year before the malfunctioning atmospheric processors finally shut down altogether. Earth technicians repaired them all, effectively stopping the doomsday clock—or pausing it for an indeterminate period. Earth doctors inoculated the populace against local diseases and the ones they'd brought with them. Earth geologists discovered rich veins of thermacite crystal. And Earth capitalists began extracting it. American workers began to arrive, enticed by government jobs with the Mars Works Project Authority, one of the many New Deal programs begun by the Roosevelt administration. British miners, many fresh from chipping coal out of the Welsh countryside, showed up *en masse*. Some were shipped to the frontier in lieu of doing hard time, a tradition dating back to the penal colonies in Australia and the Caribbean.

Of course, wherever a large influx of people occurred, crime and vice followed. So AEGIS hurriedly expanded operations to those new regions, recruiting from local populations as a tactic to make a foreign occupation somewhat more palatable to the occupied. Sensing an opportunity to advocate for her people while making a living at the same time, Sinari applied to AEGIS, aced the entry exam, and blazed through Officer Candidate School as if it were the most natural thing in the world.

"Ensign," came a baritone greeting from the large office adjacent to the dimly-lit lobby. It was Colonel Robert Stevenson, fit and muscular in his late forties, salt-and-pepper hair slicked back with pomade. He wore a blue jumpsuit uniform festooned with service patches indicative of his rank and seniority, though the sleeves were pushed up, revealing a couple of tattoos on his inner arms. Wartime trophies, she assumed. Soldiers were always doing that sort of thing.

"How'd it go with Karpis?" He waved her inside, disappearing before she could get to the door.

"He's in custody with Marshal Hu." Sinari entered, finding the colonel was already seated behind his desk. She took a chair across from him, letting her eyes take in the room. Furnishings were spartan—just the desk, a couple of molded acrylic chairs, and a steel file cabinet. A variety of citations and awards were framed on the wall, telling the story of a decade of service to the organization. A black-and-white group photo of various chiseled hero types in jodhpurs and leather jackets looked to have been taken somewhere in Earth's Mideast region, though Sinari sometimes felt it difficult to distinguish those desert landscapes from the ones here at home. A younger Stevenson gazed out from the center of the group, with the familiar half-crazed look of someone who needed the thrill of adventure as much as they required food or water. The man in the photo was more slender, with darker hair, and no frosty mustache like the man seated opposite her. The man in this office had eaten a healthy slice of life since then.

"Good," Stevenson nodded. "Maybe Henry can get something out of him."

Sinari reached into the pouch on her belt and produced the glimmering shard of red crystal from the meeting in Zola's bar. "This is what he was selling," she said, placing it on the desk blotter in front of the colonel. "We should analyze it."

Stevenson picked up the finger-length crystal and twirled it in the light of the chrome desk lamp. "I'll have Nariaal take a look."

Sinari shifted in her seat. She was in dire need of a shower and a change of clothing. "If there's nothing else, Colonel..."

"Actually," Stevenson began, "there is something." He reached into a desk drawer and pulled out a manila file folder, slapping it down on the desk in front of her.

CHAPTER 3

"**I** know you've been with the organization less than a year, but your work is exemplary."

Sinari paused, unsure how to respond. "Thank you sir?" she managed. It almost sounded like a question.

"Let me get right to the point. You know when you break a bone, it must be set in order to heal properly?"

Sinari nodded, and the colonel pressed on.

"Well, there are rumblings among the larger powers on Earth. Wounds from the last world war that never healed. Broken bones which were never set, so to speak. And mark my words, any conflict that sparks there will undoubtedly spread here, and beyond. We need to prepare for any eventuality. So I submitted a proposal to AEGIS Command."

"Proposal, sir?"

"AEGIS is founding a new division of fast responders who can be deployed on special missions across the alien frontier..."

She bristled at his use of the words "alien frontier", though she knew he didn't mean anything by it. She also knew he likely didn't understand what a loaded term it was to those people whose home it was.

Stevenson pointed a thickly calloused finger at the folder. "Understand, the Space Rangers program is not for the timid. This will be hazardous duty." He rose from his chair, and she mirrored him.

"Space Rangers," she mused aloud, amethyst eyes glinting in the lamplight.

He handed her the folder. "Elite unit with broad law enforcement powers and autonomy. Sister units are mustering on Venus and back on Earth. The job comes with a bump in pay and a promotion, if you want it."

There it was: a golden opportunity to rise within the power structure and help her people, and it could not be ignored. Sinari's vision momentarily began to swim. She feared that trying to actually read the folder's contents might result in her passing out right there in the colonel's office. Deciding to ride the high, she offered her hand, and Stevenson shook it.

"I take it that's a yes."

"That's a yes," she said. "Thank you, sir." Turning to leave, she halted suddenly and pivoted back to face the colonel. "Can I pick my own squad?"

Stevenson laughed aloud. "It's your command," he shrugged. "You have complete discretion. But don't take too long. Your first assignment is already underway." He nodded his head at the folder she now clutched in her hands. "Best get to it... Lieutenant."

His charming half-smile was still imprinted in her mind as she exited the colonel's office and found her way down a winding corridor. Passing a long window which looked in on the science lab, Sinari gave a nod of greeting to the scientist inside.

Neither human nor Martian, Dr. Nariaal was of a simian build, a huge silverback gorilla in a white lab smock and tinted safety goggles. He appeared to be welding something inside a small chrome housing, lighting up the lab in tiny blue-white flashes. He looked up briefly as she passed the window, offering a perfunctory salute with a massive hand.

Sinari's quarters resembled any average Earth apartment, and were as sparsely-furnished as the colonel's office. A simple bed, a work desk and chair, and a set of drawers built into the wall was all she required. And yet it was so much more than most of her people had. The tiny en-suite bathroom contained a toilet, sink, and shower, with a couple of plush towels draped over bracketed wall rods, and a white terrycloth robe on a hook.

Once, Mars had been criss-crossed by mighty rivers. Now, inhabitants of the Red Planet typically drew their water from two sources: atmospheric moisture condensers which provided only a modest volume, and vast aquifers deep underground, accessed by well systems. The Mars 1 starbase utilized both, the mechanism sophisticated enough to provide for the hygiene and sustenance of the city's population, as well as treating and recycling waste water. That meant a hot shower— a luxury to most native Martians—was within reach of anyone with a government job or enough cash to pay for a home hydro-processor. And a hot shower was indeed what Sinari most craved at that moment.

Shedding her street clothes along with their layer of Martian dust, she stepped into the shower and proceeded to cleanse the sand and grit from every surface and crevice. A few minutes later, somewhat revitalized, she stepped from the shower stall and donned the bathrobe, wrapping a loose fall of raven hair into one of the towels. With the corner of her sleeve, she wiped the steam from the mirror above the sink and looked into her own eyes. In the somewhat sickly bathroom light, they appeared a brighter shade of orchid.

They were eyes that had seen the last of the tribal conflicts—endless generational wars over slim resources in an increasingly failing ecosystem. Enslavement by rival factions or tribes of four-armed Green Martians. Colonizers from Earth, who had solved one set of problems, but ended up bringing their own.

The face staring back from the mirror bore the emotional weight of seeing too many of her kinfolk worked to death in the mines, or sold away to the syndicates. That pain had aged her beyond her years, and was what kept her from succumbing to the siren's call of the nightclubs—slipping away into a nightmarish existence of addiction, exploitation and crime.

But just as Earth had rescued her planet from expiration, so AEGIS had saved her from that fate. As a benefactor, the agency was... imperfect, to say the least. Yet it had provided a causeway out of almost certain doom. Sinari was no fool. She knew an opportunity when it presented itself. And when she'd first put on the blue jumpsuit of the AEGIS officer, she made a solemn vow to use her status and position to help those without.

The uniform had taken some getting used to. The one-piece jumpsuit was a navy blue nylon canvas material that was both weather-proof and extremely durable, with a hidden snap closure in front, and laminated leather pads sewn into the knees. Worn belted over a black bodysuit, the uniform included calf-high black boots, and the individual's choice of fingerless or full gloves in either black or gray. The jumpsuit's blue color was apparently chosen to match the original AEGIS Aeronautics division uniform from the previous decade, though Sinari felt it didn't make much tactical sense in a desert environment of orange, red and brown.

The whole ensemble was relatively form-fitting and provided coverage from neck to toe, which was highly unusual in her culture. Red Martians historically eschewed constrictive clothing, preferring a somewhat ancient Mediterranean style of gauzy tunics when they wore anything at all. They were traditionally quite comfortable riding their war mounts into battle with nothing but a few armor pieces on the shins, lower arms, and groin. Nonetheless Sinari had made it a point to assimilate as quickly as possible, and found she actually didn't hate the imported Earth fashion, along with its art and music. It was just some of the people she could do without.

She stared at her sullen reflection for several minutes, then finally shed the towel from her head. Draping it back over the horizontal rod, she weaved a hand through the damp, dark mass of hair, content to let it dry on its own. She padded through the climate-controlled apartment, snagging the manila folder from her desk with her free hand, and flopped onto the bed. Crawling into a cross-legged position, she flipped open the folder in front of her and began to peruse its contents.

A few potential recruits revealed themselves in the form of a handful of Earthers, a Venusian woman, and a couple of locals—although native Martians didn't generally flock to the colonial service sector. And as much as she wanted to use her rising station to aid the plight of her people, Red Martian insurgents had been known to infiltrate foreign government institutions to sabotage them from within. Despite official declarations to the contrary, Mars was under occupation. Locals had to be carefully vetted, as she had been.

Before she could delve too deeply, the alarm on her intercom chimed, drawing her attention to a small speaker in a square polystyrene housing set into her nightstand. She flipped the toggle switch to talk.

"Vohn," she greeted. There was a mechanical *click* as she toggled back to listen for the response.

"Nariaal," came the baritone reply. *"Colonel Stevenson wanted me to analyze the crystal shard and get back to you with my findings."*

She flicked the switch again. "That was fast. What did you find?" Nudging the switch back to listening mode, she waited for the simian scientist to answer. When he finally did, it sent a vague tingle down her spine.

"I think you'd better come to the lab."

CHAPTER 4

"When I was first assigned to the AEGIS Special Weapons and Ordnance Research Division—known as SWORD," Niariaal explained, holding court in the science lab, "I had only recently deciphered the Elder Martian script. With the expert help of Doctor Dorothy Starr and Commander Marissa Singh."

Colonel Stevenson stood across a white acrylic strategy table from the hulking ape scientist, arms folded across his chest. Sinari, having thrown on her uniform jumpsuit, stood in a nearly identical position at the head of the table. Nariaal's comment about the acronym SWORD made her glance down at her left shoulder. A streamlined AEGIS insignia patch showed a white down-turned sword over a red and blue shield, while three stylized gold wings extended laterally from either side. It was an update of the old design chosen for its simplicity and readability at a distance.

A partially disassembled ray sidearm sat in a bracketed stand on the table's surface, pointing toward a large sheet of aluminum at the far end of the room. A copper wire ran from the rear of the pistol's battery pack to a small remote housing with two buttons. The crystal shard from Sinari's earlier trip to Carter Flats sat next to a nearly identical crystal of a deep ruby hue.

"Deciphering the script," Stevenson observed, mustache dancing on his upper lip, "was the key to reverse-engineering tri-crystal technology."

Nariaal nodded emphatically. "Correct. We discovered the Elder Martian invaders of 1894 utilized simple but effective mechanisms based on channeling electrical current through three different types of crystalline structures."

Sinari watched as he padded on wide, hand-like feet to a black chalkboard next to the aluminum sheet and scrawled a rudimentary illustration of lightning—meaning electricity—entering one side of a crystal and an amplified energy emerging from the other side.

"With the small amount of crystals left intact by the Martians, we were able to determine the primary qualities of each kind. The amber crystal, *energite*, has an energy input-output ratio of a factor of ten to the tenth power, and with it certain anti-gravity properties. The blue crystal, *Lenzium*, named for physicist Heinrich Lenz, has an inherent positive and negative polarity, giving it attractive and repulsive capabilities. And the third crystal—"

"*Thermacite,*" Sinari interrupted. "Amplifies current into a powerful heat ray."

Nariaal nodded again. "We use it in most of our non-ballistic weapons systems," he explained. "Prior to our arrival on Mars, we did find small amounts of all three crystals on Earth. Enough to power the first wave of colonization."

Sinari winced at the word, and Stevenson noticed.

Undeterred, Nariaal pressed on. "We tried to synthesize the crystals, but were unsuccessful. Which is why thermacite mining is such a lucrative venture on Mars."

"We already know this, Doctor," Sinari snapped, leaning forward with her hands gripping the table edge. "What did you find out about the shard I brought back?"

Nariaal was used to people being impatient while he attempted to educate. He held up a massive index finger. "Let me demonstrate."

Plucking the deep red crystal from the table, he placed it into the open chamber of the pistol skeleton. "This is mined Martian thermacite," he said, picking up the remote box from the table. "This is how it normally functions."

As Sinari and Stevenson watched, Nariaal pressed the first button on the remote, and the gun framework sent the battery charge into the crystal chamber. The energy erupted from the barrel as a glowing red beam with random oscillations of electricity pulsing and circling. The aluminum panel thrummed with the heat impact as Nariaal hit the second button, stopping the beam. A glowing hole the size of a quarter revealed itself in the panel.

"Typical result of a ray weapon at close range, yes?"

Stevenson and Sinari agreed in unison.

With surprising dexterity, the ape scientist removed the dark red crystal from the open pistol chamber and replaced it with the shard from Sinari's encounter with the fence. Then he gestured toward a cluttered workbench along the side wall.

"Might want to wear some eye protection," he advised.

As the closer of the two, Sinari went to the bench and grabbed two sets of lab goggles, tossing one to the colonel. Nariaal lowered his own pair from their usual place atop his broad forehead. Sinari noticed he was standing farther away from the table than with the first demonstration, so she remained next to the workbench to watch.

"This thermacite was lab-grown," Nariaal announced, pressing the first button.

The crystal exploded with outsized force, turning the gun, the stand, and half of the copper control wire into a pile of slag on the table. A tendril of acrid smoke twisted toward the ceiling vent.

It took Sinari and Colonel Stevenson several seconds to register what they'd just seen.

"That was synthetic?" Stevenson asked.

Nariaal looked over the mangled weapon in front of him and raised his goggles back to rest on his head. "Indeed."

"So who made it?" the colonel wondered.

"Anyone privy to the technology on Earth," Nariaal began, "knows the futility of synthetic crystal."

"So it's local," Stevenson finished the thought. "What do we think? Martian insurgents?"

Sinari was livid at the suggestion, but kept her cool. "No. Locals don't have access to lab facilities to do this kind of work." She cast a withering look at Stevenson. "It's definitely off-worlders of one stripe or another."

"Fair enough," Stevenson admitted. "So who?"

Sinari paused thoughtfully. "That's a good idea."

"What is?" the colonel asked.

"No, Hu is. Marshal Hu. I'll ride out tomorrow and see if he's been able to get anything out of Karpis."

"Just remember you have a mission," Stevenson reminded.

"My mission," Sinari replied, remembering what she could from the brief glance through the folder in her quarters, "has something to do with monitoring Nazi activities out in Tempe Terra. If they're somehow responsible..."

"You think they're the ones growing thermacite in a lab?"

Dr. Nariaal pried a corner of the melted pistol from the table and flipped it over with a *clank*. "If these crystals are being sold on the black market, whoever made them *knows* they don't work, and are proliferating them to those who buy from the black market—criminal organizations and terrorist groups, anyone who has the need for weapons and who doesn't have the means or access to reputable outlets."

Stevenson tossed his goggles onto the workbench. "Of course," he sighed. "If they get enough of this faulty product into circulation, it erodes confidence in the market."

Sinari clenched her jaw. "The price on Allied thermacite goes down, workers' wages go down, everyone suffers. And Germany, who has illegal mines all over the southern hemisphere, swoops in with a better grade of crystal they can sell at a premium."

Colonel Stevenson took a deep, worried breath. "This is worse than I thought. Get some rest, then assemble your team and get underway. You're on the clock, Lieutenant Vohn. I'll file the report with AEGIS command." He paused in the laboratory doorway, throwing a quick glance at the ape scientist in the lab coat. "Thanks for the demonstration."

Nariaal offered his casual salute as Stevenson left the room.

"Yes," Sinari offered, moving toward the exit. "Thank you, Doctor Nariaal."

A sly grin washed across his mouth like rolling surf. "Lieutenant," he replied. "And by the way, congratulations."

She smiled her thanks, ducking out into the corridor, back to her quarters, and a few hours of sweet oblivion.

⊂⊃

Tana clutched the grip of the AEGIS laser carbine and took a centering breath, slowly blinking and directing her gaze to the scope bolted to the top of the chrome rifle housing.

She was about Sinari's height, slim and toned, with a complexion the color of buckskin. Her dark hair was cut in a shaggy bob that appeared almost blood red in the floodlights of the shooting range. Her eyes gleamed a gold-flecked amber through a discerning squint, her expression hard and distant. An assortment of small burn scars on the right side of her face—only visible in certain light—told of a rough-and-tumble past, full of questionable decisions and predictable violence. She wore the common blue AEGIS field uniform, a two-piece hoop and cuff earring in her right ear, and a small hoop encircling the flesh of her left nostril.

Tana was not yet thirty, but had seen three lifetimes' worth of terror and death: first, growing up poor in the slums of the Venusian capital, Amtorria; second, having to prove herself as a capable enforcer to her patron gang—in part to gain social status, while avoiding being trafficked herself; and third, watching in horror as offworld mercantile ventures invaded ancient Venusian culture, and the human scum that came with them. Nazi scum. The kind that killed indiscriminately, tortured wantonly, and traded indigenous people like so much common livestock, from horned and tailed Arboreals to winged Klangans, to the golden-skinned Gan themselves. They made the worst of the Venusian syndicates look like a church service by comparison.

Tana squinted at the streaked red-orange hues of the Martian sunset, making the patchwork of scars on her right cheek resemble a city map with roads and avenues radiating like a spiderweb from an unnamed city center. She was used to slug-throwers. Nothing matched the satisfaction of dropping a rival gangster at a hundred yards with a crack of thunder. But she wanted to remain up-to-date on the latest technology, so here she was on the range. In the golden hour. Alone.

The second generation of rayguns—at least this particular carbine model—was supposed to be practical armament for the ever-expanding AEGIS operation and their agents on the "Alien Frontier". Sidearms were a known quantity, more or less, but the weapons development division wanted something that could pack a bit more punch than models already in the field, while remaining comparatively light-weight, along the lines of the Thompson sub-machine gun. But rather than spraying 45-caliber rounds in a loud, staccato drum roll, the AEGIS 44-RCX projected a superheated beam of energy at its target with the muted sound of arcing electricity. And as such, it promised a good deal more range and accuracy than a submachine gun throwing slugs of lead.

It was Tana's job to gauge and calibrate that accuracy.

Peering through the green-tinted scope, she drew a line of sight to the paper target two-hundred meters away. On its surface was the black silhouette of a humanoid head and torso, a standard ballistics print. In this case, someone—presumably Tana herself—had painted a white swastika shape on the center of the face.

Her index finger drifted down the contour of the stock and guard to the trigger itself. Aside from its chrome exterior, the carbine was strictly no-frills. A skeleton shoulder stock extended from the back, leading to an electric battery pack above and behind the trigger assembly. The battery connected to a circular thermacite crystal chamber, which amplified the small voltage by extreme orders of magnitude. This compounded energy was channeled through transparent resonating coils in front of the trigger, ultimately focused through a flared barrel about 45 centimeters long.

Tana took another calming breath, keeping the reticle stationed over the hand-drawn swastika in the center of the target's head. Exhaling into the approaching night, she muttered, "So long, Fritz," and caressed the trigger.

There was no recoil. Just a cycling electric hum as the chrome barrel emitted a beam of sizzling red light. It only lasted a second, although she knew she could have sat there all day until the thermacite crystal failed or the battery pack died. Her finger pulled away gracefully, and she saw in the green light of the scope that the shot had seared a crispy hole through the center of the target's head, with no portion of the swastika remaining.

Looking up from the weapon, she realized the mischief she could get into with one of these beauties.

Yes, she thought. *This will work nicely.*

CHAPTER 5

Sinari slept hard and rose early, leaving the starbase behind in a cloud of dust. She revved her Triumph back along the desert road to Carter Flats, a blue streak zipping past rocks and the desiccated corpses of scrub plants. She still had a squad to assemble, and had begun to pore over some of the personnel files over her morning coffee—thanking the Goddess for another sublime Earth import.

To say there was a dearth of quality candidates for her squad would have been an understatement. And yet, there were a couple of promising recruits. She planned to start interviewing the moment she got back from seeing Henry Hu.

She arrived in the mining town after most of the workers were already gone, thus the streets were as empty as they'd been the previous day. The wind had kicked up, blowing small clouds of dust and stinging sand over the wall from the deep desert. Those who were outdoors wrapped themselves in cloaks, goggles, and scarves against the nuisance, and were invariably headed toward shelter of some kind.

Sinari pulled the motorcycle to a stop in front of the marshal's office and killed the dynamos, dismounting at the same time. She waited until she was standing inside the office to shift the driving goggles to her forehead, pull the cowl beneath her chin, and lower the poncho's hood to rest on her shoulders. Glancing at the cell to her right, she could see Karpis resting comfortably on the cot, an aluminum meal tray picked clean of the Salisbury steak and peach cobbler. The boiled green beans were untouched.

The marshal was sitting at his desk, and beckoned her closer. "What happened at HQ?" he asked.

"Good morning to you too." Sinari moved to the front of the desk and parked her hip on it. "The shard was lab-grown. Oh, and I got promoted. This case is now an official mission from AEGIS Command."

"Well, congrats, Vohn." Henry raised an eyebrow and smiled. "Is that Lieutenant now?"

"It is," she smirked. "Gotta fill out a squad, deadline yesterday. If you're interested…"

Marshal Hu leaned back in his chair with a thoughtful look. "I like you, Vohn. But the agency pays me to look after this little colonial neighborhood. Not enough, to be sure, but honestly, I've grown to like it here." He winced as if ashamed to confess it. "Just the same, I'm happy to keep working with your squad of…"

"Space Rangers," she finished. "It's a new elite division, special law enforcement powers on the frontier."

"Space Rangers, huh?"

"Yeah. Kind of sounds like a comic strip, or a radio show."

"It does at that," said Henry.

Sinari shifted her weight as she threw another glance toward the jail cell. "Did you get anything from Karpis last night?"

Henry leaned forward, hands folded on the desk blotter in front of him. "A bit, yes. You know, when you first started looking into this, we were both thinking it was going to be fragments of mined crystal stolen from the companies."

"Right," Sinari nodded, leaning her left arm on the desk for balance. "But it looks like the mined crystal has dried up on the black market, and replaced by this synthetic stuff."

"Yeah, well there's a reason for that. Seems the Nazis have been buying up all the real crystal as well as harvesting their own. Meanwhile they're pumping these fake crystals into circulation, causing confusion in the marketplace."

"To what end?" Sinari wondered, and the answer dawned on her as Marshal Hu spoke the words.

"They're trying to corner the market on natural thermacite, put legitimate suppliers out of business, and come to the rescue with their own supply—at a premium. Or they just hoard them for their own munitions."

Sinari's amethyst eyes narrowed to slits. "And if their artificial crystal ends up in enemy weapons, so much the better."

The marshal sighed, leaning back again. "Exactly."

Sinari cocked her head toward the cell. "What are you doing with Karpis?"

"He's being deported back to Earth for prosecution. FBI's been looking for that joker for three months."

The door burst open, and a hooded figure stepped in from the whistling wind outside. A man of average height, wearing protective goggles and a dark gaiter obscuring his face from nose to chin. He was dressed in dust-covered military fatigues and wore a sidearm at his hip —a chrome weapon of decidedly AEGIS design.

Marshal Hu rose from his chair, and Sinari watched as the stranger pushed a male human in front of him, gripping the back of his collar. The smaller man was shackled. He stood upright of his own accord, but was decidedly the worse for wear. Clothing dirty and torn. Eyes caked in sand and dust, face looking like worn leather. The stranger's left hand held a cargo net which he hauled inside with some effort, dropping the contents in a pile and pulling the door shut.

"Got another one for you, Marshal," the stranger said, words muffled through the woven material over his mouth.

Henry gestured toward the empty cell beside the one containing Karpis. "Put him next to our guest," he ordered.

Sinari slid from the desk and stood watching, arms folded in a pose more curious than defensive. The stranger manhandled the smaller fellow into the second jail cell and uncuffed him while the marshal set a decanter of drinking water next to a washbowl on a table near the cot. The men exited, leaving the prisoner to recover from his forced journey. Karpis stirred from his slumber and took notice of his new neighbor as Henry locked the cell door behind them.

As the two returned to the office, the stranger pulled down his own hood and gaiter, raising the goggles to rest on his forehead. Sinari blinked as she took in the sight. His hair was dark chestnut, cheeks taut with wind and sun. His jaw, though bristling with several days of beard, was strong and angular. He fixed her with the deepest of blue eyes, drawing a folded piece of paper from his belt.

He was far more attractive in person than the photo in his personnel file. She decided he was probably the most ruggedly beautiful Earth man she'd ever seen.

"Bobby 'The Jackal' Meyer," he said in a sprawling Liverpudlian accent, unfolding the WANTED poster and slapping it on the marshal's desk. "One thousand U.S. dollars."

Henry reached into his desk drawer and pulled out an official form, scrawling data in various boxes. As he did so, the stranger turned to Sinari and offered his hand.

"Ensign Drake Dawson," he said. "AEGIS."

Sinari shook his hand formally. "Lieutenant Sinari Vohn," she replied, sure that he could tell her affiliation from her jumpsuit with the AEGIS insignia on the shoulder.

He gave a quick salute in deference to her rank, but she was already pressing on.

"You get a bounty on top of your pay?"

Drake flashed a charming smile, eyes dancing in the dim light of the marshal's office. "It's from the mining company," he explained. "That's why I leave the federal cases to other agents. Draw a paycheck and get the corporate bonus. Cake, eat it, etcetera."

"Seems like you've given some thought to how to game the system," Sinari quipped, wondering if it would get under his skin.

"I've been gaming the system all my life," Drake replied curtly. "Only way to survive, where I come from." He glanced around the office, noting the marshal's progress filling out his paperwork. He wasn't a fan of smalltalk, and hoped they could wrap up the clerical stuff as quickly as possible. Just the same, the presence of the other prisoner piqued his interest. "I see someone brought in Creepy Karpis?"

Sinari adopted a tough stance with hands on hips to take up space. "That's right," she smiled.

Drake did a double-take, realizing the implication. That meant this Red Martian woman wasn't just a token local recruit to put on a show for the natives. The thought that she might be not only competent but *excellent* forced him to recalibrate his first impression. He was now intrigued. "Well done, Lieutenant."

Marshal Hu finished filling out the form and scribbled what passed for a signature at the bottom. "Here's your voucher," he said, handing the paper across the desk to Ensign Dawson. "Don't spend it all in one place."

"Never do," Drake replied, folding the document and shoving it in a snap-pouch on his belt. "I stick it all in the bank."

"What's that?" Sinari asked him, indicating the cargo net near the door. A variety of what looked like mechanical limbs, scrap metal, and perhaps a medium-sized spotlight were tangled up in a pile.

Drake moved toward the door, looking down at the bizarre catch. "Not sure yet. Found Jackal near a crashed vehicle in the desert. He had this thing already bagged up and waiting in his truck. I was going to bring it back to the lab and let the ape have a look."

Sinari bristled. "*The ape's* name is Doctor Nariaal, and he outranks us both, so show some respect... Ensign."

"Fair enough," Drake replied immediately, holding his hands at chest height in surrender. "Too right, Lieutenant. I apologize. Been out here by myself for too long. Easy to forget the real world."

"Maybe that needs to change," she said. "You being out in the desert alone."

Drake squinted his sapphire eyes, puzzled. "Ma'am?"

"You said Jackal had a truck?" Sinari began, laying out her plan bit by bit.

"Yes, ma'am. Crossley troop truck. Parked outside."

"How about you give us a ride back to headquarters? I'll fill you in on the way."

Drake looked confused. "Us?"

Sinari gestured toward the first jail cell, and Henry grabbed his ring of keys from the wall to retrieve the prisoner. "You, me, Karpis, my bike, your... whatever's in the net. It would be easier than me having to officially commandeer the vehicle."

Drake smiled. She was direct, to the point, and able to improvise. He liked that.

"Yes ma'am," he said, giving a slight bow and gesturing toward the door. "Your chariot awaits."

CHAPTER 6

Drake Dawson steered the Crossley along the same stretch of packed desert earth Sinari had made into a habit over the past days and weeks. He listened to the lieutenant describe the new Space Rangers program as she kept an eye on the shackled prisoner on the bench in the back. The heavy canvas cover flexed and puffed over the metal ribs straddling the truck bed, buffeted by the moaning wind. Sinari's motorcycle, strapped to the bench opposite Karpis, bobbed and bounced with every jostle of the suspension. The metallic contents of Dawson's cargo net likewise clicked and clanked as the truck rolled on toward the Mars 1 starbase.

"Let me get this straight," Drake began, hands gripping the wheel. "You think Nazis are growing dummy thermacite in a lab somewhere?"

Sinari glanced through the rear window at Karpis, realizing he couldn't hear much, due to the rumbling road noise. "That's the theory," she said. "I've been tasked with putting a unit together to investigate."

"Good pitch," he replied. "I'm in."

Sinari cast a dubious look at him. "Just like that?"

"Well, I figure it's easier if I just volunteer," Drake looked over at her with a cocky half-smile that threatened to disarm her well-cultivated social armor. "Save you the paperwork of having me transferred in."

"You could always dispute a posting," she said, pondering his logic.

Drake shook his head. "No. No I can't," he explained, shaking his head. "You see, I didn't exactly 'enlist'. I'm here under somewhat... shall we say... unique circumstances."

Sinari had seen mention of some trouble back on Earth in his file, but she wanted details. "Explain?"

Drake reached up to scratch a fleeting itch on his nose. He kept his eyes forward, watching the road stretch out ahead of them. "I... was sent here in lieu of prison."

Sinari narrowed sparkling purple eyes, but she didn't flinch. "I read something about that."

"I grew up in Newsham Park—it's an orphan asylum in Liverpool, England," he explained, squinting straight ahead.

Sinari nodded along with his story. She had proximate knowledge of England from her interactions with British scientists, miners, and administrators on Mars. "What happened to your parents?" she asked.

Drake shrugged. "Dunno. Welsh on my dad's side, given my name. Might've been a coal miner, or sailor. Never knew my mum." He cleared his throat as the truck churned a trail of road dust in its wake. "Anyway, not a lot of mobility at the bottom of the social ladder. Not in the United Kingdom, anyway."

"I'm familiar with that," Sinari sighed.

Drake stole a quick look and returned his eyes to the road. He hadn't yet considered what her story might be, and if it was perhaps similar to his own. "Yeah?"

"Yeah. But go on."

"Well, I ended up in front of the magistrate more times than I can count. Just petty crime, stealing to live. Until it wasn't."

"What did you do?"

There was a long silence while Drake put his answer together. "Stepped in to break up a scrap. Mate o' mine was getting right duffed up. The other bloke cracked his bonce on the curb and died."

Sinari wasn't sure what a "bonce" was, but context told her cracking it was a fatal injury. "Sounds justifiable in defense of your friend."

"You'd think, but..." Drake wiped a bead of sweat from his brow, returning his hand to the steering wheel. "The bloke in question was a bobby—er, a police officer."

Sinari knew the implications when it came to law enforcement. The disproportionate value some lives were given over others had always seemed unfair somehow, and was compounded by some using their status and authority to exploit and abuse others. "I see," she said quietly. "So you were charged—"

"With murdering a cop, yeah."

They drove in silence for several moments before Dawson spoke again. "So I was looking at hard time in Dartmoor, but someone high up in AEGIS Command apparently saw some value in shipping me out to the frontier. And here I am."

"Here you are." Sinari gave him a thoughtful look and was about to follow with a smile when there was a crash from the rear of the truck and Karpis disappeared from her view. She heard herself bark an order to stop the truck, but Dawson was already down-shifting to a rolling halt.

Sinari burst from the passenger door and cleared the tailgate, taking a visual scan of the interior: her motorcycle and the net full of scrap were still inside, but the metal peg which once secured the manacles to the truck bed had been pried loose.

The desert wind screamed across the highway, blasting everything in its path with stinging particles of sand. Even so, she could make out a hobbling silhouette about a hundred meters distant. She'd have to make this fast.

She lowered her goggles over her eyes with one hand, and pulled her sidearm with the other. "Stay by the truck!" she shouted over the howling wind.

Dawson skidded to a stop, raygun already drawn. "Are you sure?"

"I'll be right back!" she shouted, waving him away and running into the storm.

Sinari regarded the windstorms of Mars much like someone native to arctic climes tolerated snow and ice. It was an ever-present feature of the biome, something she'd spent her life acclimating to. But these desert tempests were strong by any standard—even to Terrans from arid environs.

Without eye or breath protection, Karpis couldn't run far. She found him not two hundred meters north of the road, on his knees, blind, choking on a mouthful of sand. His hands were still cuffed in front, with the steel chain connecting them to the manacles on his ankles. She wouldn't need to use force to subdue him—the desert had done the job for her.

Holstering her weapon, Sinari clutched the back of his collar and began to haul him backward across the sand, much like Marshal Hu had done the previous day.

Dawson met her at the truck, and together they hoisted their prisoner back into the bed.

"I'll ride with him," Sinari said. "We can finish our chat later."

Drake gave a perfunctory salute and climbed back into the cab. As the truck started up and rumbled away, Sinari shook her head at Karpis, disappointed.

Alvin Karpis spat a wad of wet dust from his lips and managed that off-putting sneer of his. "Sorry, doll. I had to try."

"If you say so," she sighed. "I'll be happy when you're on the next rocket back to Earth. Then you'll be someone else's problem."

The rest of the drive was quiet save for the rumble of the truck on the road. The wind eventually died down as the dust storm moved on to the northeast. It was mid-afternoon by the time the Crossley entered ASA Mars 1. Karpis was put in a holding cell at AEGIS headquarters pending transport home.

While Sinari oversaw her prisoner's processing, Drake Dawson hauled the bulging cargo net to the science lab, delivering its contents to Dr. Nariaal for examination. The two reconnected briefly in the hallway, headed for their respective quarters. Drake had several days' worth of desert on him, and was in dire need of a shower and a shave. Sinari had her own bathing agenda to see to, followed by a more in-depth study of Dawson's file. They made a plan to meet up for dinner, at the very least to complete the earlier conversation, and discuss the current mission. He had said, after all, that he was in.

She had her first official recruit.

CHAPTER 7

The city lights were already flickering on when they made their rendezvous on the concrete steps of the ASA complex. Sinari dressed tastefully in a dark skirt and sport coat, with low-heeled lace-up ankle boots. A large beret draped over her left ear. Drake, freshly shaved, cut a handsome silhouette in a twill suit, gray fedora cocked roguishly on his head. A pair of well-worn black wingtips shuffled on the stair. If not for Sinari's distinctive red skin tone, they could have been any Earth couple out for a night on the town.

Drake turned, offering the crook of his arm. "Ma'am," he muttered out of habit.

"Thank you," she said, somewhat surprised at the formality. They descended the stairway together to street level and headed east. Sinari wasn't quite used to the social mores of Earth people, though she was quick to adapt. From antiquity to its not-so-distant past, her culture had been patriarchal, with only a small amount of social mobility for women. But in recent generations, a population decimated by disease and war had become far more egalitarian out of necessity—and that was the world in which she'd come of age. She found herself amused by these gestures that struck her as "chivalrous", especially given that, in a dangerous encounter, she was equal to any man.

"I know of this nice little place," Drake said. "Decent food, good music. That is, if you're not sick of jazz."

Sinari's eyes danced in the glow of the street lamps along the sidewalk. "I love jazz."

The sun finally set before they finished the four-block journey to Red Harlem. The neighborhood was alive with the sounds and smells of nightclubs and ethnic restaurants serving everything from Italian to Chinese, falafel to curry, Creole cuisine to Zodangan barbecue. Muffled strains of lively dance music seeped from the smoky clubs into the street, songs overlapping and bleeding into one another as they walked. Sinari inhaled the earthy aroma of tikka masala from a nearby Indian bistro, happy to be back for the first time in months.

Drake led her to a windowless nightclub lit with neon that read THE CANYON CLUB. She'd sampled many of Red Harlem's offerings, but she'd never actually been inside this place, despite admiring the warm glow of the marquee from time to time. The proprietors had chosen a somewhat kitschy Old West motif, the interior walls and booth alcoves adorned with painted storybook scenes of the American frontier. They were about as historically accurate as a western shoot-'em-up matinée at the cinema, but since most of the patrons—Sinari and Drake included—had never been to the American west, nobody much cared.

A jazz band conjured lively dance music from a half-moon stage edged with incandescent footlights, in front of a mural of a southwestern desert sunset. Aside from the cacti scattered here and there, it could have easily depicted Mars.

A Lebanese maître d' in a white dinner jacket beckoned them to a booth overlooking the dance floor and left them with a pair of menus. Drake doffed his hat, hanging it on a coat hook on the wall next to the seat. They settled in as a waiter arrived to take their cocktail order—a Salty Dog for Sinari, an Old

Fashioned for Drake—and soon found themselves looking across a candlelit table at each other. It suddenly dawned on both of them what a ridiculously romantic setting they'd chosen.

"Nice place," Sinari said, breaking the tension as she glanced around the club, taking in the sharply-dressed wait staff and dancing couples crowding the floor.

"The house band is decent," Drake replied with that alluring half-smile, "and they pour an honest drink."

"We'll see," she winked.

They perused the food options in silence for several moments.

"Ever been to the Cat's Meow?" Sinari asked, absently scanning the appetizer listings.

"No, where's that?"

"Two blocks west. More of a dive than this place, but the band is hot, and talk about an honest drink..."

The waiter returned with their cocktails on a tray, which he tucked under his arm as they ordered dinner. When he was gone, Drake leaned forward, the candlelight from the red glass lantern casting conspiratorial shadows on his otherwise charming features.

"I'd normally insist we go after we're done here, but I think we have business to discuss."

"Agreed."

Drake waved a hand across the table, inviting Sinari to speak. "So please... discuss. You were saying in the truck that you're familiar with the plight of the working class."

"Oh, I am." Sinari ran a slender finger thoughtfully across her lower lip. "My people have these glorious legends of ruling warlords and heroic deeds, but look where centuries of almost constant war got us, not to mention plague and famine—which always hits the poor and laborer classes so much harder."

"So we share a similar background," Drake mused, taking a sip of his Old Fashioned from the whiskey glass. "Hooray for class solidarity. Now, what can you tell me about this mission?"

Frowning at the dearth of words taking shape in her mind, she took a sip of her own drink. "I don't know where to start. I've been commanding this unit for about a day."

"That's as good a place to start as any," he said. "How many in the unit?"

"One," she answered, a bit too quickly. "Well... two, including me."

Drake blinked in disbelief, and Sinari caught his expression.

"What is it?"

"Well... I'm *good*," he smirked, leaning back in the booth, "but we're gonna need some more bodies. Y'know, don't wanna hog all the glory."

Sinari gave a throaty chuckle. "I know that, Ensign. I've had command for exactly one day, remember? Haven't had much time for recruitment."

"Right."

"I figure Dr. Nariaal can be our technical liaison. Wouldn't want to take him away from his precious laboratory."

Drake took a swig from his Old Fashioned and pursed his lips at the tangy mix of bourbon and orange bitters. "Although... have you seen him? He'd probably be quite handy in a fight."

"Apparently he saw some action back on Earth, but I don't know the details. I'll definitely invite him, though."

Drake pondered a moment while Sinari mentally paged through personnel files. "If you need a crack shot," he said somewhat hesitantly, "I might be able to make a recommendation."

Sinari looked back at him expectantly. "Who?"

"Tana," he said before glancing away nervously at the dance floor.

Sinari caught his hesitation. She'd run across that name in the personnel files, but hadn't had a chance to dig any deeper. "Venusian?" she tentatively recalled.

"That's the one."

Sinari recalled the file photo of a slender woman with sharp features and dark hair cropped in a bob. "What can you tell me about her?" The question was open-ended enough to entice him to speak at length, but it was his body language she was most interested in. Dawson's initial nervous reaction had piqued her curiosity, and she wondered what else he would give away.

"From what I understand, she used to be an enforcer for one of the local Venusian cartels. A real tough bird, that one..."

He trailed off, and Sinari realized that was all she was going to get. From what she knew of organized crime on Venus, one would have to be tough to survive in that world of trafficking and violence. "You say she's a crack shot?" Sinari asked, probing for more clues.

"Helluva crack shot," Dawson said, finding her gaze with a granite expression and those impossibly blue eyes. "Bullet or laser, makes no difference."

That one look told her everything. They'd slept together. She was sure of it.

"Any hesitation working in the same unit?"

Dawson cracked that handsome half-smile again. "Well I won't speak for *her*, but there's no problem on this end."

An electric moment passed between them, and each immediately found something else to look at.

Dinner arrived, and that was the end of shop talk for the evening. They enjoyed steaks carved from imported Terran cattle, with mixed greens and fingerling potatoes. Another round of drinks followed, along with more harrowing tales of childhood trauma, each insisting the other's story topped their own.

Sinari and Drake found in each other an easy partner in conversation, some witty repartee, and more than a little sexual chemistry—though neither was willing to act on it. At least not there and then.

They worked off their dinner on the dance floor. The band played a full set of popular swing jazz tunes, which were wildly popular with the local Red Martian clientele, and the two newly-minted AEGIS Space Rangers added the Foxtrot and Lindy Hop to their skill sets.

When they stepped from the Canyon Club into the street, still buzzed from all of the "honest drinks", Red Harlem nightlife was still going full throttle, despite the late hour. Terran miners and service workers sauntered with their Martian counterparts, chatting animatedly against building exteriors or flitting from bar to nightclub and back like honeybees hunting nectar. Drake and Sinari backtracked along the sidewalk, taking a short detour through an alley to make up some time.

They didn't notice the thug until he was blocking their way.

He looked to be human, perhaps of Mediterranean background, with thin strands of greasy black hair poking out from a crumpled porkpie hat. Dressed in the manner of a street-level gangster, pinstripe trousers and a matching vest over shirtsleeves and a crooked bow tie, he stood just over a meter and a half tall, none of it very substantial. However it wasn't his physicality which gave them pause, but rather the tommy gun he held across his body. "Evening, folks," he greeted with a sinister grin, pulling the bolt back on the Thompson with a familiar ratcheting sound.

The two halted in place, instantly sober. Drake held his hands up in surrender, but sent Sinari a hushed instruction from the side of his mouth.

"Back out to the street."

"No good," she replied, throwing a glance over her shoulder behind them.

"And why's that?"

Sinari turned sideways to keep the smaller gunman in view, while allowing Drake to see the mountainous Green Martian blocking any hope of escape. "...Him," she said, gesturing with a thumb.

The brute was the color of ripe avocado flesh, nearly three meters tall, the yellowed ivory of his mandibular tusks sharpened to savage points. All four massive fists were wrapped in chains. He filled the alley, creating a rather convincing barrier to their escape.

"Don't make it more difficult than it's gotta be," warned the greasy thug in the vest and tie. "Cash is all we're after."

Sinari squinted at him. Of the whole situation, the man's bow tie, cocked at ten and four o' clock, bothered her the most.

"Nobody needs to get hurt," Drake agreed, reaching to his lapel in full view.

The gangster raised the Thompson's barrel to point at Drake's chest. "Easy, pal. Nice and slow."

Drake nodded, slowing his motion. Sinari glanced down at his left hand, which was hanging at his side. His first two fingers crossed and uncrossed in quick succession.

Her eyes widened as she realized his intent. *He's not...*

"Here," Drake offered, reaching into his jacket. "Take this..."

CHAPTER 8

Drake produced a billfold from his inside breast pocket, and made sure the thug with the tommy gun was tracking it with his eyes.

Sinari watched, simultaneously cursing and admiring his impulsive instinct as she reached inside her own lapel, ostensibly to get her own pocketbook. Her impression of time seemed to slow as her situational awareness surged, and her vision became saturated with vibrant color—even within the shadows of the dank alleyway.

The thug followed Drake's wallet as he reached out with it.

The brute pressed the fist of one dominant arm into the palm of the other, dropping the second pair of arms to his sides.

Sinari's fingers grazed the cool metal of the object within her jacket.

And Drake let the wallet slip from his hand.

The thug's gaze dropped with it as it fell to the ground. Before it slapped to the street, Drake landed a solid uppercut with his right, his left hand grasping the barrel of the Thompson.

Sinari conjured a small raygun about half the size of her normal sidearm and trained it upward at the Green Martian's face. "Back off," she commanded, as Drake slammed his right forearm against the thug's windpipe, sending him sprawling to the dusty concrete.

The fight was over before it began.

The brute took a step back, unused to the very notion of a mark putting up any resistance whatsoever. It was usually so easy. They'd only been working this neighborhood for a month, but it was a completely new experience just the same. While his boss choked for air, this Red woman brandished her hold-out pistol in his direction, and the Earth man covered the alley with the stolen tommy gun.

The towering alien took a tentative step toward his boss, then reconsidered as the

Thompson barrel raised in concert with the raygun.

"Don't," Sinari warned.

Both sets of massive green arms returned to the alien's sides.

"Now, we're going to be taking your associate in to be booked," she explained. "And because I don't have two sets of extra-large cuffs on me right now, I'm gonna let you choose."

The Green Martian looked at her expectantly, as Drake shifted the submachine gun barrel toward the thug.

"You can cause trouble," Sinari said, as if ticking off a list, "and we'll subdue you and take you in. Or you can come in voluntarily, which makes our job easier, but something tells me you're not *that* loyal to your partner here."

Drake squatted down, rolling the thug onto his belly and frisking him with one hand, as the man continued to cough and gasp for breath.

"Or, your third option," Sinari continued. "You back out of here and find yourself some legal employment. Something not cartel-enforcer-related."

The brute stood frozen in place as he processed the choices in his head. Then, nodding, he backed out of the alley and disappeared into the night.

Drake removed a .38 revolver, a blackjack, and a wallet from the would-be robber, standing upright to share his findings with Sinari. "You strap a Bee-Sting?"

"Never know when it'll come in handy," Sinari smiled, replacing the holdout pistol in her shoulder holster.

Drake passed her the wallet and stashed the revolver and sap in his own jacket. "Controversial, letting Big Green and Ugly go like that."

"Not if you don't report it," was the deadpan reply, as Sinari rifled through the wallet's contents, beginning with his ID. "Atticus Bianchi. American citizen."

The would-be mugger stood, snarling. "Yeah, and I know my rights, ya crazy broad!"

A solid punch square in the nose from Drake sent him back to the ground, and was enough to shut him up.

Sinari continued to rifle through the contents of his wallet, not bothering to even look at him. "You threatened two law enforcement officers with deadly weapons and tried to rob them. Just keep talking, friend. It's all going in the case against you."

The man began to say something, then opted to cradle his bloody nose in silence.

Sinari unclipped a folded stack of bills and fanned them to check the denominations. "Looks like there's a bit of everything here. Martian scrip, American dollars, British pounds... and German Reichmarks."

"Our man doesn't discriminate," said Drake as he hauled the thug to his feet. "What now?"

Sinari paused, re-folding the money and slipping it back inside the wallet. "Let's get him back to headquarters, book him."

When Sinari had mentioned not having extra-large manacles, she'd omitted the fact that neither she nor Drake carried cuffs of any kind in their civilian clothes. So they walked Bianchi the half dozen city blocks back to the AEGIS offices at the spaceport, and locked him in a holding cell for the night.

The two parted outside the security area, each of them joking about knowing how to show the other a good time. Drake shuffled off to his spartan quarters, Sinari to hers. She wasn't certain, but there was a persistent tug at the back of her mind about the Reichmarks in Bianchi's wallet that went beyond the odds of him having recently robbed a German tourist. There was something else, something deeper. A connection to her current mission that couldn't be ignored even if she'd wanted to.

She decided she'd pull that thread and see where it went, but it would have to wait until she'd reset herself with a decent night's sleep. A sleep that unfortunately never fully arrived. She tossed and turned, kicking fitfully as she dreamed—a crimson thread which unraveled from a distant rectangular shape as she continued to tug at it. She pulled, and more thread unwound and coiled at her feet as the massive shape edged closer to view.

After what seemed an eternity, she could finally see it in full as it hovered into a sourceless light. The thread she pulled was unraveling a giant flag.

A red field, with a black swastika symbol on a white circle at its center.

The flag of the Third Reich.

❧

The trucks rolled into the village center just after nightfall. Polished headlamps lit up the modest tribal town as four Opel Blitz cargo trucks rattled to a halt, forming a semicircle under the desert sky. The trucks were painted in a desert camouflage scheme, with canvas covers displaying a large swastika on each side. The thunderous clomp of boots hitting the ground put a stop to the drunken bacchanal in the open plaza.

The mood among the native folk sobered instantly, and they turned their collective focus to the party crashers—twenty German troops in desert fatigues. Tribal warriors stood from tables and benches, mystics turned hooded heads. All hands went to the nearest weapon, willing to draw if necessary.

The Nazi troops formed a second crescent in front of the trucks, silhouetted by the glaring white beams of the headlights. They stood in place with ray carbines at the ready.

A tall, well-muscled Martian strode fearlessly to a point between the soldiers and his gathered people, hand resting on the pistol at his hip. He wore his black hair in a fade with the top kept longer, a style imported from Earth. His chosen wardrobe was canvas and leather, of a type favored by guerrilla fighters in Spain, and his skin showed a dusky clay hue in the ambient light. This would be his thirty-fourth summer, his second as chieftain. Instinctively, he chose the spot to confer with whomever these visitors revealed as their leader, and stood waiting.

Several moments passed, with both sides frozen in combat readiness. Finally, the crescent of soldiers split in the middle to allow another dark figure to step through. Though his face was obscured by shadow, the man wore a long coat and officer's head cover, and strode with purpose toward the tribal leader awaiting him.

"Ich bin Jared Lur von Long Canyon," the chieftain announced in heavily accented German, the presumed language of the soldiers in the trucks displaying that particular symbol. He was about to add, "guardian of the Aoolian Plain," when the man in the long coat raised a pistol and, without a second of hesitation, gouged a hole through his head with a laser blast.

The tribe had been frozen in readiness. Now they were frozen in shock and fear.

Jared's body hit the dusty ground, head smoldering.

The man in the coat rested a boot on the corpse, holstering the weapon he'd just fired, an act of supreme bravado. He knew these people primarily understood English as their secondary language, and he was fluent. "I am Dr. Rotwald," he said with a slight Bavarian lilt, "and I represent the German Reich. The soldiers behind me are Waffen-SS. The finest on the alien frontier."

The clan waited in silence, still collectively reeling from the execution they'd all witnessed just seconds ago.

The man continued: "I have need of able bodied laborers to assist in some very important work. If you come without resisting, you will be treated humanely, and you will be paid for your labor."

A warrior among the gathered tribe made a subtle move to draw a sidearm, and the Nazi soldiers stepped forward, powering up their rayguns in a unified mechanical hum.

"If, however, you choose to take up arms against us, you will suffer the fate of any who defy the Reich. Your village will be razed, and every last man, woman, and child will be exterminated. Your history will be lost. Your bloodline wiped from the universe. The Long Canyon tribe will have never existed."

The man in the long coat who spoke from the dark stood patiently as the warriors of the Long Canyon consulted each other in silent glances which spoke volumes. Ultimately, those of working age dropped their various weapons to the ground and stepped forward in submission.

CHAPTER 9

Dr. Nariaal wiped the machine oil from his broad hands, casting the utility rag to the top of the the pile accumulating under the work bench. With those same massive mitts, he coaxed the sleeves of the white coat down to his wrists from their earlier position near his elbows.

He didn't see Tana until she was already leaning in the doorway.

"All-nighter?" she asked.

The ape scientist regarded her from his rolling stool. "Just finishing up on a new project," Nariaal replied in his gravelly baritone. He shrugged out of his lab coat, revealing a jumpsuit the same blue color as Tana's underneath. Padding a few steps on wide simian feet, he hung the coat on a hook next to the counter. "Were you summoned as well?"

Tana nodded. "Any idea why we're being called in this morning?"

"I haven't the foggiest notion, but it may very well have to do with Lieutenant Vohn's special assignment."

Tana raised an eyebrow. "*Lieutenant* Vohn?"

"Yes, what is it, Ensign?"

The reply came from directly behind her and made her jump. Tana spun to see the copper-complected Sinari Vohn, freshly showered and clearly already caffeinated, leaning against the wall in an approximation of how Tana had been standing just a moment ago. Her AEGIS field uniform was pressed and clean, sporting a new set of blue and gold Space Rangers patches—one on the left chest, one on the right shoulder. She held a stack of manila folders tucked under her arm.

Tana frowned. How was Vohn able to sneak up on her like that? *Nobody* was that stealthy. At least nobody she'd ever encountered. And she'd been mob muscle in the Venus underworld. She was *used* to people trying to catch her unaware.

"I—I uh..." she stammered, "I got a message to report to the conference room for a meeting?"

Sinari nodded. "I sent that."

"Just making sure there's not some kind of mistake."

Drake Dawson rounded the corner and strode toward the group. Dressed in a clean one-piece uniform of navy blue, his gait betrayed a gleeful swagger. Whatever their first mission threw in their direction, it would be more fun than tracking bounties through the Martian desert. "No mistake," he said. "I may have sung your praises... a bit."

Tana's head was suddenly full of questions, and Drake decided the bewildered stare she gave him was well worth getting up earlier than usual.

Sinari watched the exchange without feeling the need to elaborate just yet. The corner of her mouth curled up in a wry half-smile, and she angled her head toward the open doorway across from the laboratory. "Shall we?"

The four entered the conference room, Sinari taking up the rear and marveling at the bulk of Dr. Nariaal's shoulders as he negotiated his way through the door.

"We have a lot to do, and not a lot of time to do it in," Sinari began, "so I'll get right to it."

She turned to shut the conference room door, and when she circled back around, all eyes were on her, staring in rapt attention.

She wasn't used to command. And while she'd often been the object of attention—usually the wrong kind of attention—more often than not it was devoid of the respect she now found herself receiving. This was a brand new experience, and it wasn't altogether unpleasant.

A nervous sort of energy pulsated throughout her body, so she decided to stand, which would also reinforce the sense of authority she wanted to cultivate. She recalled the clan chieftains from her childhood had two universal traits. The first was natural charisma, something that was inherent and couldn't be learned. The second was a way of claiming their physical space in the way they stood and moved. It was as if every step they took was taking a hill and winning a battle. She tried to put that into practice ever day.

"We've discovered that someone... Nazis... are flooding the market with artificial thermacite."

Tana raised a calloused but graceful hand. "I'm sorry, *artificial thermacite?* Is that even possible?"

Sinari flashed a brief look at Dr. Nariaal, who nodded solemnly.

"It is," she answered, "and they have. And it behaves just as you'd expect."

"By exploding?" Drake queried. "I'd expect it explodes."

Sinari sighed. "Putting it mildly, yes, it explodes."

Nariaal held up a finger, adding, "And turns both weapon and user to melted slag."

"Gods of the sky," Tana muttered.

"Our mission," Sinari continued, "is to figure out where the contraband is being made. The crystals have to be grown in a lab. We need to locate that lab, and shut it down, by any means necessary." She leaned over the conference table, urgency written in her expression. "You are here in this room for a reason. Some have past mistakes to pay for. Some are looking for a new challenge. Some want to serve the greater good. I know I'm a little from each column. It's just us right now, and we'll have to make do with the gear and supplies we have on hand. But if we can complete this first mission, I know that AEGIS will put more resources into these operations in the future."

Tana cast a curious glance at Drake, who returned it with with a wink.

Sinari saw the silent exchange. "Tana, I understand you're a pretty good shot."

The compliment, while undersold, drew Tana's attention back and she shrugged in a token show of modesty.

"Never seen better," Drake offered, his eyes straight ahead. Tana's golden cheeks flushed pink.

Sinari continued: "I've read your stats. Glad to have you backing us up." She folded her arms and stood back from the head of the table. "Tana, Drake, and I will spend the majority of our time in the field, while Dr. Nariaal provides laboratory and science support back here."

"Where do we start?" Drake asked.

Tana folded her hands thoughtfully on the table. "I know of a small-time trafficker here on Mars, used to run slaves to the Venusian cartels. And we know the Germans operate illegal crystal mines in both northern and southern hemispheres. If they're buying slave labor, he probably has an in with them."

Sinari squinted at the revelation. "Who is this gangster?"

"He's a Gan, from the Mypar kingdom. Had a compound in Para-Tuun. Ran a pretty successful operation, until he crossed my former boss and got himself banished, minus a couple of fingers."

Sinari leaned over the table, jotting some notes on a pad lying among the file folders. "Great connection. What's his name?"

"'Jamar the Gold'. Or at least he used to be. Here, he's known as 'Jimmy Two-Fingers'."

Drake stifled a laugh. "That's just precious, that is."

"That's a really good start," Sinari affirmed. "I think that's our way in." A building sense of excitement was cycling around the table, and she knew she'd have to temper expectations. She leveled a grave look at the occupants of the conference room, her tone solemn. "Look, this is going to be a pretty rag-tag operation to start, until we can show some results. If any-one doesn't want to be here, I need to know now."

The directive was met with stony silence, as she'd hoped. "Good. Any questions?"

Tana raised her hand once again. "When do we get to kill some Nazis?"

Drake followed Tana's lead. "And what's the hazard pay like?"

"You'll get a bump in your normal salary," Sinari answered, turning to address Tana's question with an audacious twinkle in her eye. "As soon as we find where they're making the crystals." She scanned the room a final time. "Anything else?"

All eyes roamed from face to face, but no one spoke further.

"Outstanding," Sinari smiled, tossing a handful of embroidered patches identical to the ones on her chest and shoulder onto the table. "Welcome to the Space Rangers."

CHAPTER 10

The plan was set: Tana would make contact with Jimmy Two-Fingers and set up a meeting. He apparently had a penchant for Red Martian women, and Sinari would make a tempting specimen. The meeting would have to take place in a neutral location; taking control of Jimmy's lair after presumably being disarmed upon arrival was a challenge to massive to consider with only three Rangers on-site.

Tana would try to talk Jimmy into meeting in Carter Flats. It was proximate to Mars 1, and they'd have Marshal Hu for backup.

The tan Venusian excused herself to make the call. As the rest of the group prepared to disperse, Dr. Nariaal held up a broad hand.

"Lieutenant Vohn, I'd like to show you something in the lab." Then he turned to Drake. "It concerns you as well, Ensign."

Sinari exchanged a look with Drake and waited by the exit for the simian scientist to lead the way.

Nariaal took them into the work area, to a corner filled with various industrial tools and diagnostic machines. Things with switches and gauges and all manner of complexity—complexity which usually gave Sinari a headache, but which Dr. Nariaal embraced with abject glee. In all of their interactions, he'd either been taking something apart, putting something together, or holding a lecture on how he'd done one of the two.

At the center of this workspace sat something vaguely humanoid-shaped, its details obscured by the drop cloth which covered it.

"Ensign Dawson," Nariaal addressed, "where did you say you found the salvage you returned with Bobby 'The Jackal' Meyer?"

Drake's brow furrowed as he recalled. "Out near Tempe Terra, about sixty kilometers east of Carter Flats. But Meyer could have had it for some time before that."

Sinari frowned. "What is it, Doctor?"

Nariaal began to answer, but decided to let the object under the cloth speak for itself. Taking a corner of the canvas in one hand, he drew it gently away, revealing a mechanical construct unlike anything any of them had ever seen.

It was seated on a work stool, but Sinari estimated it would stand about one and a half meters tall. It's "head"—she assumed it was a head anyway—resembled a light one might find on a movie set in Hollywood: a cylindrical metallic casing focused outward through a single convex lens for an eye. A sinewy neck formed from cables and armatures descended into a torso that was somewhere between mechanical and organic-looking. Its arms mimicked the design of the chest, with graceful lines punctuated by primitive servos and hydraulics. Each hand was equipped with two padded fingers and a thumb, while each foot was a broad, two-toed platform with an articulated heel.

"So that's what all that junk was," Drake mused under his breath.

Sinari bit her lower lip. "What *is* it?" she repeated.

"That remains to be seen, Lieutenant," Nariaal shrugged. "I didn't want to power it on until you could be here."

Drake scratched his head. "Looks like a robot of some kind?"

Nariaal nodded in agreement. "Its internal systems are all very intuitive and conventional in the way they were designed. But its external construction is something I don't think we've ever seen on Earth."

Sinari crossed her arms in apparent discomfort. "Mars and Venus didn't have any kind of robotics before trade with Earth, and the Lunari are still a primitive culture. So where did it come from?"

Nariaal paused, and Sinari knew instantly what he was going to say before the words left his mouth. "Why don't we ask it?"

Sinari held up a hand to stop him. "Hang on, Doctor. I assume you've made sure this thing isn't some sort of weapon?"

"I've found nothing in its circuitry or mechanical construction that I would define as *inherently* dangerous," Nariaal answered, adding, "but science is the process of seeking answers in an unknown universe. And we arrive at those answers through experimentation."

Drake cast a look at Sinari that said, *"let's go for it,"* and she found the risk to have a certain appeal. *What's the worst that could happen?* she thought. *Famous last words.*

"Okay," Sinari sighed. "Do it. Switch it on."

Nariaal moved to the side of the robot and reached toward its back. There was a *click*, and the lens in the middle of its head lit up immediately with a blue neon glow. The chest compartment began to whir with internal activity as servos went to work. Although it remained seated, the head jerked up, alert, and began tracking back and forth, taking in the room's interior and the people in it.

"Query," came a gentle but masculine tone with an electronic filter, as though speaking through a radio not quite tuned properly to the station. "What is my current location?"

Sinari dropped her arms to her sides to appear neither defensive nor aggressive. "You are in the laboratory at AEGIS headquarters at the Mars 1 spaceport."

The robot head scanned up and down as she spoke. "Mars," it repeated. "Thank you." It paused momentarily as calculations whirred and clicked inside its processors. "Additional query: what is... AEGIS?"

"AEGIS stands for the Allied Enterprise Group for Interplanetary Security," Sinari explained. "I am Lieutenant Sinari Vohn, of the AEGIS Space Rangers." She gestured toward the others, adding, "This is Ensign Drake Dawson, and Dr. Nariaal."

The single eye roamed from face to face, scanning and registering them in turn. When it turned to the side and took in the great go-rilla frame of Dr. Nariaal, the robot gave a brief spasm of... was it surprise?

"Summary," it chattered aloud to the room. "Martian female. Terran male. Simian primate of unknown origin, male."

"I'm Terran as well," Nariaal stated in his booming baritone.

The robot head did a double-take, clearly not expecting humanoid speech from an ape.

Nariaal turned to Sinari. "It apparently has a basic internal memory core that was left un-damaged. That's promising."

"Meaning what, exactly?" Sinari wondered.

Nariaal thoughtfully ran a massive finger along his jaw. "Meaning it can register differ-ent types of entities in the local space, and know what they are. I didn't program that."

"Query," Sinari cocked her head and folded her arms again. "What is your designation and origin?"

There was a pause as the construct's inter-nal processors hummed. Finally it mirrored the angle of Sinari's head and offered the best answer it could muster. "Declarative: I am Zed. Origin..." the electronic voice trailed off, gears and circuits buzzing. "Origin is..." It fi-nally stopped, as if taking a breath. Its me-chanical body language adopting one of curious resignation. "Apologies. Origin is... unknown."

"You have no record of who made you?" Sinari pressed. "Or why?"

"Negative," the soft robot voice admitted. "I have no memory prior to this time. Only my designation."

"Your designation—'Zed'?"

The robot whirred in response. "Zed. British pronunciation of the last letter in the English alphabet."

"That was me, actually," Nariaal explained. "It required a designation in order to initialize its processor."

Sinari pursed her lips in thought. "I see."

"Its operating and computational systems were a blank slate," said Nariaal. "It could have encountered an electromagnetic field of some kind, that may have damaged its short-term memory."

"Possible," Zed nodded. "That would explain much."

Drake shifted in place. "It was in pieces in the back of the Crossley," he recalled. "Seems like it was more than just an electromagnetic field."

"I was?" Zed asked, its canister head craning back in surprise. "That is not ideal."

Drake stifled a laugh at its reaction. "No. No, your condition was... not ideal."

"But you brought me back here?"

"Yes," Drake nodded. "I thought there might be something more to the pile of parts I found."

The robot turned to focus on the gorilla scientist. "And you repaired me?"

Nariaal nodded as well. "Affirmative."

"Thank you," the robot offered. "Thank you both."

Drake wasn't sure how to react to electronic gratitude, but Nariaal responded on his behalf.

"You're welcome."

Sinari's head began to fill with questions, but one seemed to rise above the rest. *Can this thing be an asset to the mission, and if so, how?* She turned to Nariaal. "Is this... Zed... robot... thing... can it be programmed?"

"It can," Nariaal nodded. "Whoever made it included a keypunch card interface."

Sinari squinted at the robot. "Good. Get it set up with some standard support tasks, subject to the AEGIS command structure. See how it does. If it works well, we might be able to use it in the field." She nudged Drake with an elbow. "Sorry. I know it's technically your salvage, but I'm commandeering the robot for AEGIS business... for the time being, anyway."

Drake was unfazed. "Commandeer away," he said with a wave. "I've no use for a robot."

"Carry on, Dr. Nariaal," Sinari instructed, striding to the exit. "Come with me, Dawson. We have to bag a mobster."

CHAPTER 11

Tana had to sift through some leads before she was able to track down Jimmy Two-Fingers. But once she got through to the gangster, it was fairly easy to talk him into a meeting. He was initially surprised to hear from her—it'd been a few years since his exile from the Venusian underworld.

She explained that she, too, was an outcast from the Venus syndicates, and had some success dealing in Martian contraband. She wanted a connection to the crystal market, and had a source for Martian "laborers"—a quaint euphemism for *slaves*. Tana described a wide variety of sectors her personnel could fill, from menial labor to domestic, to the sex trade. And that was all it took. Jimmy's preference for Red Martian women was well-known. He was, as those in his circle said, a sucker for the Reds.

With the meeting set for the following day at high noon, Tana and her companions set to work planning their first official Space Rangers operation.

They would meet outside of Carter Flats, in a small canyon a mile north of the main road. Tana would have only her Terran enforcer and the bidding item, one able-bodied Red Martian female. Jimmy would have a single bodyguard of his own.

Tana wanted five thousand British pounds, but Jimmy offered twice that amount in Martian scrip, with the option to decline the merchandise on appraisal, and she couldn't very well decline either point.

Drake followed Tana's lead in regard to dress. They had to appear tough, but not desperate. Nor could they wear clothes that were too upscale and flashy. They settled on a wardrobe cobbled together from surplus military fatigues and native desert wear, complete with leather boots and the hooded ponchos so popular with locals.

Sinari opted for something comfortable to fight in if need be, yet revealing enough to entice Jimmy's primal appetites. An embroidered linen halter criss-crossed her chest, while a matching loincloth hung hip to knee. Arms and legs were bare, displaying an athletic tone and decorated with tribal glyphs painted in shimmering gold pigments. Open sandals reached to mid-calf, strapped with gold accents and brown leather. Her raven tresses were brushed loose around her shoulders, with two thin, beaded braids framing her face.

Very little of her body was left to the imagination—in ancient times, Red tribesfolk often wore little to nothing, save for the display of jewelry or armor. But over the past couple of generations, the cultural trend had leaned a bit more toward modesty. And when the Terran powers arrived, with their post-Victorian sensibilities, the native population gradually adopted the mores of practical clothing. Sinari's outfit spoke of compromise between the two. She looked as though she could have been a bride of her grandmother's generation. And as such, there was little available real estate in which to secret a weapon of any kind. She chose a pair of hammered gold bracelets with matching arm cuffs. A small dagger could be hidden inside the bracelet on each wrist. It would have to suffice.

Drake and Tana opted for slug-throwers in terms of personal armament. Rayguns were relatively new technology, generally only available to law enforcement and the military, while conventional pistols and rifles were still the tool of choice among the criminal element. Mars had a long tradition of superior ballistic weapons, the planet's lower gravity and air density making for longer ranges and more accurate shots. Tana selected a Martian slug pistol that resembled an elegant, hand-engraved Luger, while Drake packed a .45 automatic from the armory.

The last thing Sinari did before climbing into her bed was make a short radio call to Marshal Henry Hu in Carter Flats.

❦

The team piled into the Crossley an hour after sunrise, Drake navigating the truck to their chosen destination, Tana riding with Sinari in the back. It took a couple of hours to arrive at the canyon's coordinates, but they were still early for their rendezvous. This, of course, was by design. Sinari wanted to have an opportunity to survey their surroundings before Jimmy Two-Fingers showed up.

As it happened, Jimmy Two-Fingers had the same notion, and had arrived fifteen minutes before them.

The Venusian gangster stood next to his enforcer, watching the Crossley's approach with great interest. He was lanky, with sun-tanned golden skin a similar shade to Tana, and dressed in a familiar combination of military surplus and local desert wear. Instead of a full poncho, he wore a hooded mantle over a long khaki duster. As the truck pulled to a squeaky halt, he pulled the hood down, revealing a shaved head and manicured beard clipped in the Van Dyke style. Multiple gold earrings glimmered in the dim canyon light.

Drake stepped from the cab and waited patiently for Tana to round the back of the truck with their commanding officer in disguise. He exchanged a polite nod with Jimmy and his goon—a Terran in ragged fatigues and a few days' stubble on his chin.

Tana emerged from the rear of the Crossley with Sinari in tow. Glancing up along the canyon ridge, she noticed a few convenient vantage points for Jimmy to have stationed a sniper. She naturally assumed he had, but she wasn't worried. They had their own ace in the hole.

"Tana, me girl," Jimmy saluted as the two women approached the meeting place. "Been a long time." The Venusian gangster looked appraisingly at the copper-skinned woman walking silently a few steps in front of Tana. "What'd you bring me?"

Tana smirked, the subtle scars on her cheek crackling into a grid. "As promised, I brought you some ice cream. Nodding at Sinari, she added, "I know you like strawberry."

"You remembered," Jimmy replied, undressing the Red Martian with his eyes—not that there was much to undress. "I'm touched."

Sinari kept her gaze as low as possible, while engaging her other senses with their surroundings. Her initial survey told her that Jimmy was about her size, though slightly heftier, and he was favoring an injured right leg. So far, he maintained an easy demeanor, a passive stance. Of course, she reckoned that was a well-practiced façade. Beneath the surface of civility, he was prepared for anything.

But then so was she.

"Come here, darling," Jimmy beckoned. "Let me take a look at you."

Sinari cast a brief glance upward at the canyon ledge, and Jimmy caught it.

He immediately reached toward the holster at his hip. Before he could draw his sidearm, Sinari sloughed free of the loosened manacles, drew two small blades from their housings in her golden vambraces, and spun behind the gangster with one at his throat and the other poised at his kidney. "No, Jimmy," she muttered, "let's take a look at *you*."

The enforcer went for his pistol, but halted in mid-lurch when he saw Drake's automatic pointing toward his chest. Dawson shook his head "no" in warning, and the thug raised his hands to shoulder level, sighing in resignation.

Jimmy twitched under Sinari's grasp, throwing a desperate look at the ridge. "Fire, Brooks! Fire, damn you!"

A brief whistle echoed down the canyon walls, and Sinari could make out the form of Marshal Henry Hu, bush hat and duster silhouetted against the morning sky, rifle resting sideways across his shoulders.

"Hey down there!" Henry's voice found them on the canyon floor. "Brooks isn't feeling so good. He's gonna take the day off."

While Drake disarmed the goon, Tana went to frisk the boss, discarding an eclectic assortment of weapons in the dirt at his feet.

"I'd like you to meet Lieutenant Sinari Vohn," she said, nodding toward the woman holding Jimmy at knife-point. "AEGIS Space Rangers."

Still clutching the gangster from behind, Sinari breathed across his right ear. "Charmed, I'm sure."

"A-AEGIS?" he muttered, brain trying un-successfully to piece together the puzzle. The initial shock finally wearing off, his face re-laxed somewhat. "Tana, me girl. What's this all about? Are we still cross over the deal at Jhanshin?"

"The one where you took off with ten cases of Hadal whiskey without paying for it, and left me to explain the matter to my boss? *That* deal at Jhanshin?" Tana looked over a 9mm Luger from the pile on the ground. "Looks like you've been doing some business with the Nazis." She passed the gun to Sinari, who re-turned the blades to her wrist cuffs.

"Sure," Jimmy admitted. I do business with everyone. Americans, British, Ger-mans..."

"They're not *Germans*," Drake corrected. "I know some Germans who are rather decent people. You trade with *Nazis*."

Jimmy glanced from face to face. "What's your point? What do you want?"

Sinari moved in front of him, holding the Luger at his belly. "We want you," she said softly, with a wink, "to do some more business with the Nazis."

There was a long silence, while the gang-ster contemplated her meaning. "You looking for Black Market contacts? Because I'm happy to—"

"We want to meet your counterfeit crystal supplier," Sinari demanded. "You hook us up, AEGIS might look at forgiving some of your more heinous transgressions... like trafficking people."

"Hmmm. Let me think..." Jimmy paused, thoughts whirring away like an electric clothes dryer. "If I refuse?"

A sly grin broke across Sinari's face. "We take you in, you get booked for every last crime. Possibly even deported back to Venus."

The look of abject terror that washed over Jimmy's face told Sinari everything she wanted to know. Death—or worse—awaited him back home.

He would do it. He would work with them. She was certain of it.

"I'll do it," he said finally. "I'll work with you."

Sinari chuckled to herself. *Amazing,* she thought. *I think it, and it comes out of his mouth.*

CHAPTER 12

Sinari knew Jimmy wasn't a man who put much stock in verbal contracts, so she loaded the mobster and his enforcer—an Armenian named Garen—into the back of the Crossley to keep them safely under supervision at AEGIS headquarters, while Marshal Hu held Brooks in a cell at his office in Carter Flats. The would-be sniper was a surly ginger whose freckles livened up an otherwise granite countenance. He scowled all the way into the cell, but he never uttered a word. And that was just fine with the marshal.

After Jimmy and Garen were photographed and fingerprinted by AEGIS admin, they were fed and provided with a well-appointed and well-monitored lounge in which to await further direction. A large picture window dominated one wall, overlooking the bustling spaceport. Two sofas and a couple of chairs were arranged in a U-shape, interspersed with acrylic end tables and a few potted ferns. It reminded Jimmy of the lounge at the Lyric Hotel on Venus. He hated it. And by extension, he hated this room too.

When the Rangers re-joined them, they were in uniform. And this time, they were joined by a fourth. Jimmy and Garen both blinked as if to wash Martian dust from their eyes.

Was that a gorilla?

In a lab coat?

"You know," Jimmy pressed, "my boys are gonna start wondering what's holding us up."

Sinari offered that disarming half-smile that seemed to diffuse most any awkward situation. "Don't worry, Jimmy. We won't keep you long. Just need you set up a meet with your Nazi contacts."

Jimmy and Garen exchanged a wary look, which did not go unnoticed.

"What's wrong?" Tana wondered.

Jimmy shrugged. "We're gonna need a good story," he explained. "Rotwald can see through a lot of flea dirt."

Tana knew he wasn't talking about tiny Earth fleas, but the giant variety indigenous tribes domesticated and used as mounts in the deep swamplands of Venus. The amount of dung they produced was legendary, and usually ended up heating entire jungle villages.

"Rotwald," Sinari repeated. "Is that your contact?"

"Doctor Karl Rotwald?" Nariaal interrupted in a booming bass that caused Jimmy and Garen to jump in collective surprise. "He's in Research and Development for Himmler's elite SS division. 'Special Projects', they call it."

"That's him," Jimmy acknowledged. "He's the one running the thermacite lab operation."

"Do you know where the lab is?" Sinari wondered.

Jimmy shook his head. "Not the exact location, but we make our buys out near the Long Canyon."

"Long Canyon?" Sinari repeated. "He's here? In the north?" This was the first she'd heard of a Nazi operation anywhere in the northern hemisphere, and it filled her with simultaneous dread and excitement.

Jimmy nodded.

"And you're selling his shite to the Allies, knowing it blows up," Drake snarled.

"It's just business," Jimmy shrugged, pleading his case to Drake, who he could tell would have pummeled him if not for the uniform he wore, and the witnesses in the room. He'd have to watch that one carefully.

"Not anymore, he's not," Sinari corrected, locking eyes with Jimmy from across the room. "And if he doesn't want to get delivered back to the Venusian syndicates, he's going to make a special introduction."

Jimmy's mind was racing again, trying to find an angle from which to negotiate. "Like I said, you're gonna need a good story."

Sinari opened a manila folder and handed Jimmy the third sheet from a carbon copy set of papers.

"What's this?" he wondered.

Sinari winked. "It's a purchase order from a very legitimate import-export concern here in Mars 1. Looking to supply the U.S. Army on a government contract."

Jimmy scanned over the document. It looked legitimate. He passed it back to her. "He'll only take cash. In your case, American Dollars."

"We can handle that," Sinari assured him. "How much for a half-ton of lab crystal?"

Jimmy did a quick calculation. "Ten thousand should do," he answered, adding, "Plus ten percent for my commission."

Drake had to will himself to hold a certain instinct in check: the instinct to punch Jimmy squarely in the face.

"There's something else," Jimmy said. "He's got between fifty and a hundred SS troops defending the operation. They're not hirelings. They're true believers."

Tana's face showed granite resolve. Her golden eyes burned. "Bring 'em on."

Drake flashed a look of matching intensity. "Too right."

"Tell you what," Sinari countered. "You do this for us, and in addition to expunging the most serious offenses off your record, I'll throw in a small bonus." Her tone suddenly became ominous. "But remember—this amnesty isn't permanent. You get caught in any serious violations in the future, I'm not lifting a finger to save your miserable Gan hide."

Jimmy had clearly pushed this Martian as far as she would go, and his criminal gut told him she wouldn't budge further. And she was serious about the consequences. "Understood," he nodded.

Sinari shuffled the carbon copy back into the folder and looked Jimmy dead in the eye. "Now make the call."

☙

Jimmy placed a radio call from Mars 1 and a meeting was set. The proposed deal was ten crates of raw, lab-grown thermacite for ten thousand US dollars. A small introductory exchange to establish the relationship.

They congregated on a small plateau at the mouth of the canyon at Tempe Terra, over four hundred kilometers to the northeast. Close to the Nazi lab, but not close enough to pinpoint its exact location, which is how Rotwald wanted it.

Sinari's public-facing team consisted of herself and Drake Dawson, now posing as part of a black market syndicate. Jimmy was on hand to make the introduction, with Garen as his muscle, just as in real life. Meanwhile, Tana took up position on a dusty rock shelf in a cliffside half a kilometer east of the meeting spot. A vintage Martian bolt-action slug rifle was her chosen companion for the day. The last thing she wanted was to advertise her position with a beam of red-hot light.

She slid back the bolt on the rifle, chambering the first round from the spring clip in the bottom. Then she popped open a portable tripod mount and set it in front of her, near the edge of the rock shelf. Locking the rifle onto the tripod, she scooted into position with the hand-carved shoulder stock braced against her pectoral muscle, and peered through the scope to take in the scene.

Dr. Karl Rotwald was a scholarly-looking man in his forties, with graying temples and round wire-rimmed glasses. He was of average stature, clad in the standard brown desert cammo fatigues of the German *Army*, flanked by a small unit soldiers in similar dress. Their uniforms were topped off with the ever-present mountain cap, each with the stylized eagle of the SS pinned to the front. Tana took note of the rifles each soldier carried slung: some sort of energy carbine, of an unfamiliar make.

Behind them were parked three Opel Blitz trucks—1934 models, probably. Two were clearly meant for hauling passengers, while the third was stuffed with wooden crates marked *ACHTUNG - EXPLOSIV*.

As Jimmy led his entourage forward from the Crossley, a dozen or so Red Martian laborers shuffled to the back of the cargo truck, ready to begin unloading at Rotwald's order.

They appeared to be wearing metal collars of some kind.

"*Guten Tag, Herr Doktor,*" Jimmy hailed in German. "As promised, I have some new buyers for your product."

"*Guten Tag,* Jimmy." Rotwald paused, squinting at the foursome. "They have brought my money?"

Sinari tensed. *Did he just say 'MY money'?*

She exchanged a look with Drake, who apparently had a similar thought, though he ultimately shrugged it off.

Jimmy gestured to Sinari, who stepped forward, clutching an aluminum briefcase. "This is Dasha, representing Red Planet Exports. Dasha, say hello to Dr. Rotwald."

Sinari drew up on Jimmy's right, giving the German scientist a formal nod. "Good day, Doctor." She offered the case. "Perhaps this will make the day even better."

Jimmy smirked at Sinari's improvised dialog. It was a nice touch.

"Good day, *Fraülein.*" Dr. Rotwald gave a slight bow, but that was to be the end of formal good behavior. "Kindly open the case?"

Sinari was expecting caution. He'd never met her before, didn't know who she was, or what she might have inside that metal briefcase. She'd do precisely as he did, were their positions reversed.

"Absolutely," she acknowledged, popping the clasp on the front of the case, and raising the top. "Care to count it?"

The bundles of currency inside were real, and Rotwald knew it. "Not necessary," he said, waving a dismissive hand. "If you short me today, there will be no future business. I know that is not what you desire."

His attitude was extremely casual, almost flippant, and Sinari did not like the salacious undertone when he said "desire".

Rotwald motioned to the Red Martians by the cargo truck. *"Die Fracht übertragen!"* he barked.

Immediately, the slaves began unloading—two laborers to a crate—in a procession to the back of the Crossley. Sinari watched with barely hidden disgust. One of the flanking soldiers approached, taking the case from her hands.

"I know our boss is interested in your operation," she added hopefully. "Perhaps we could have a look sometime."

Jimmy winced. *Don't push it, girl.*

On the rock shelf, Tana scanned the meeting below through the rifle scope. So far, so good. In fact, it had gone smoothly enough that it made her just a tad nervous. There was so many moving parts, so much that could go wrong. It was only a matter of time before this whole operation blew up in their faces—she was sure of it.

She suddenly felt precarious, as though she *wasn't* well-hidden halfway up a canyon wall with her back to solid rock. This wasn't right. Something was off. Some small factor they hadn't considered.

A feeling in her gut flared like a Roman candle, and she knew she had to get the hell out of there. They all had to get out of there.

The soldier stepping around the corner of the canyon path had other plans. A single stun shot from his raygun caught her mid-torso as she scrambled to stand, and everything went black.

On the ground, Dr. Rotwald heard the muffled electric sound of the shot. All heads turned toward the canyon wall.

Sinari looked back at the Nazi scientist, who met her gaze with absolute fury.

"Alarm!" he bellowed, and chaos answered the call.

The desert exploded in shouts, bullets, and laser beams.

CHAPTER 13

The air around them was instantly angry—and on fire.

Drake could only hear the electronic *zap* of the German ray guns, a short expletive from Sinari, and Jimmy screaming as he ran in the opposite direction. Before he knew it, his own sidearm was in his hand and firing, dropping three soldiers in mere seconds.

Sinari ducked away behind Garen as Rotwald retreated toward the first truck with his adjutant and ten thousand dollars in cash.

What in the name of the Goddess happened?! she wondered as energy beams lit up the canyon. *Whatever it was, we're in the fire now. The real trick will be getting out alive.*

This time, she'd brought her AEGIS-issue ray pistol, along with the tiny holdout. She drew both and began blazing away, double-fisted. The Bee-Sting was only effective at short range, which—fortunately or unfortunately—was precisely the environment they were in. The pistol was well-suited for maximum carnage in close quarters.

Two more shots fired. Two more Nazi soldiers dropped to the desert floor, smoldering holes in their chests.

She hadn't been in many firefights, but she remembered one rule above anything else: *aim for the center of mass—nothing fancy.*

"Fall back to the truck!" Sinari hailed, pulling Garen by his sleeve, only to feel him drop to the ground moments later. Glancing down, she saw Jimmy's bodyguard was missing half his face, and the other half was charred like a piece of wood. Cringing at the horrible sight, she stepped away from the body and wove a path toward Drake, dodging streams of searing light.

The soldiers continued firing in a staged retreat toward the troop truck as the Martian laborers dived for safety behind any obstacle they could find. Red-hot beams flashed back and forth across the canyon. One slave caught a stream of lethal energy across his torso as he turned to flee. Another shot scarred the

Crossley's hood next to Sinari's shoulder, and another three plowed furrows in the ground by her feet.

Where's our cover fire? she wondered. In answer to her own question, it dawned on her that something must have happened to Tana—perhaps the very thing that touched off this powder keg, and suddenly everything became so much worse.

We thought we were so sneaky, so clever having Tana on overwatch, she thought. She realized their success using the marshal at the earlier meeting with Jimmy had spoiled her. This was Rotwald's turf. He knew the canyon and its environs as well as any local. How dare she be surprised that he'd outmaneuvered them?

Deep breath, Sinari. Learn and move forward. She flinched as a hot beam of light flashed by her cheek. *Well, not literally forward,* she clarified in her mind. *Stay behind cover!*

Sinari took up a firing position behind the Crossly's bonnet and targeted Nazi troops as they backed away. Now that they were beyond the Bee-Sting's range, she put the holdout pistol away and used her primary weapon to pick off what soldiers she could.

A hand on her shoulder made her flinch, and she turned to see Drake at her back. With a fraction of her tension dissipated, she fired a laser blast across the hood of the Crossley, dropping yet another Nazi soldier. It seemed like no matter how many she killed, a new one would take its place, presenting a fresh target. In her heart of hearts, she knew it wasn't merely metaphorical. As long as bitter, ignorant men were able to be radicalized, there would always be more.

Drake crouched at her hip, aiming low around the the front bumper. "What now, Lieutenant?" he asked while emptying his magazine at the fleeing troops, realizing too late that he was at a disadvantage with his conventional sidearm versus energy weapons with a practically infinite number of shots. The only reloading a raygun needed was the occasional crystal replacement or popping in a fresh battery pack. Usually with weeks or months of dependable use between each swap.

Sinari felt herself freezing up. The Nazi scientist had fled the scene with all of her seed money, and his soldiers were about to escape in the second troop truck. Meanwhile three crates of lab-grown thermacite sat crated in the rear of the cargo vehicle.

The bad thermacite!

After all, she had to do *something* to salvage a bad situation so she could grab Jimmy and Tana and get the Seven Hells out of there.

Adjusting her aim to the crates remaining in the bed of the cargo truck, she offered Drake a quick aside. "Keep down!" she warned, and he shifted backward a step.

Her focus narrowed and her heartbeat surged in her hears as she squeezed the trigger.

The crate went up in a superheated fireworks display, reducing the cargo truck to an abstract sculpture of melted slag. The explosion slammed the troop truck over on its side as its fuel tank ruptured and immediately caught fire. The screams of immolating soldiers trapped in the back echoed across the desert, as a handful of Red Martians found discarded weapons and proceeded to target individual Nazis trying to escape the flaming wreckage.

They didn't see it as slaughter—they saw it merely as restoring balance.

Sinari made no move to stop them. In her mind, it was actually a small mercy. She would just as soon let them cook.

A warm wind blew through the canyon, carrying the road dust from the wake of Rotwald's vehicle as it vanished in the distance.

Drake stood, loading his last spare magazine.

Sinari stepped from behind the front of the Crossley and took in the scene. Two smoldering vehicle wrecks. The corpses of shot or roasted Nazis littering the canyon floor. A half dozen dead Martian slaves—now eternally free.

Drake found Jimmy cowering under the bed of the Crossley, and hauled him out by his collar. He was about to ask his lieutenant what she wanted to do with him, but saw that she'd begun a conversation with the liberated Martian survivors, and felt it was probably unwise to interrupt.

The former slaves gathered around Sinari, one of their own, speaking in the indigenous tongue. There was some nodding, some pointing and sundry descriptive gestures, and a general murmured affirmation. Then the group disbanded with whatever weapons they'd scavenged from the dead soldiers, and wandered into the desert on foot.

Drake was still holding Jimmy's collar when Sinari returned to the truck, her face a mask of grim concentration. "That looked like a productive conversation," he said with a raised eyebrow.

"I told them they were free to take the soldiers' weapons and return to their clans," she explained. "Most of them are local to this region. They'll be home by nightfall."

"And a few more Martian civilians have energy weapons," Drake mused quietly, but loud enough that Sinari heard.

"And...? What's your point, Ensign?"

Dawson's face went passive. "Nothing," he offered. "A satisfactory outcome all round." Hoping to diffuse the tension a bit more, he shoved Jimmy slightly forward. "Found this trash under the truck. What are we doing with it?"

Sinari put the still-warm barrel of her raygun under Jimmy's chin. "I'll look after him while you take a look up there on the shelf to see what happened to Tana."

Drake Dawson was only too eager to extricate himself from the somewhat tense exchange with Sinari, so he gave a curt nod and released Jimmy's collar. He headed toward the cliff side at a quick amble, looking for the trail Tana had used to wind her way up to the outcropping.

"She's either dead, or they've got her," Jimmy muttered cryptically.

Sinari jammed the pistol further under his jaw, forcing his head backward. "Shut up, Jimmy. The more you talk, the fewer reasons I have for keeping you alive."

Jimmy Two-Fingers was not one to take advice to heart. "Look," he said. "We've all faced setbacks in business. We can still walk away from this."

"You might have a thing for Martian women," Sinari spat, "but you clearly don't know our tenacity. Our ferocity when the situation is dire." She drew within inches of his face, her eyes drilling into his own. "And if you don't shut your damn mouth, you're gonna find out firsthand."

"So you're not going to let me go?"

Sinari almost laughed aloud at the feeble attempt to weasel out of a situation she had no intention of letting him weasel out of. "No, Jimmy. I'm not letting you go. You're mine for the duration. If you stray from the path, if you so much as *breathe* in a manner I don't like, you're getting locked away in a dark hole somewhere, or sent back to the syndicates on Venus. And by the Goddess, I don't give a desert rat's backside what they do with you."

Drake was only away for a few minutes before he returned to the truck, panting from the climb. Sinari watched him jog to a stop, giving him a few seconds to catch his breath in the thin air.

"It's as bad as we thought," he said. "Maybe worse."

"What happened?" Sinari demanded, her grip tightening like a vice on Jimmy's arm.

"Tana's gone," Drake explained. "The Nazis have her."

CHAPTER 14

"That was damn sloppy," Sinari muttered as she climbed into the cab of the Crossley. "I should have assumed Rotwald would have troops everywhere to keep snipers from becoming a factor."

Drake frowned. "Too right. But none of us thought of it either."

"You're not in command of this outfit," she snapped. "It's not your job to think of it. It's mine."

Drake started the truck and nudged it into gear. "You're being too hard on yourself."

In the canvas-covered bed, Jimmy Two-Fingers sat in contemplation on the bench, staring at two crates of artificial thermacite.

He cringed with every bump and jostle, half afraid the kinetic motion would set off an explosion like it had back in the canyon, and half wanting it to happen.

They set in for the long drive back to the spaceport, and Sinari and Drake each decided independently of one another that, should Tana survive this encounter with the Reich, they owed her a drink. And so much more.

Sinari knew in her gut that the time for sneaking around was over. The Nazi scientist had her made, and she resolved that she would never be outgunned again.

No, the next time, they'd take grav sleds or hover cycles, and all the firepower they could muster. If the Nazis had a laboratory full of unstable thermacite, she would use it to bring the entire mountain down on top of it. On top of them all, if necessary.

It was almost evening by the time they returned to Mars 1 and Jimmy was placed in a temporary holding cell until Sinari decided what to do with him. Preparations commenced almost immediately for a return, and with more resources.

Drake traded in his .45 for an AEGIS ray pistol—a new model that Nariaal had been developing. It had a sort of teardrop-shaped barrel with light emitting coils visible below the chrome shell and fit his grip comfortably. He also dropped his undercover garb in exchange for his blue AEGIS jumpsuit.

Sinari changed wardrobe as well, slipping into her blue uniform and requisitioning some special equipment from the armory: a couple of those new ray carbines.

Then she went to visit Jimmy Two-Fingers in his holding cell behind a shimmering transparent blue Lenzium field. "I need to know where we stand," she said, dispensing with any pleasantries whatsoever.

Jimmy squinted at her from a bunk at the back of the cell. "I'm fine, thanks for asking." His upper lip curled with the sarcasm. "It's now been over a day since you picked me up. My gang is gonna be wondering where I am, and with whom."

"What goes on between you and your gang isn't exactly my main concern at the moment. I need to know where we stand. Especially with Rotwald, but also between you and me."

Jimmy rose wearily to a standing position, rubbing his temples with the sheer effort of thought. "You and me?" He gave a bemused chuckle. "Me girl, there is no *you and me*. There's *me*, getting bent over for every last bit of use I might have to the colonial government. And there's *you*, doing the bending, with your ambition, and your agenda. Despite the fact that I never caused you any harm."

Sinari marveled at his mental gymnastics. "Jimmy, you were all set to sell me into the sex trade—probably after using me, and/or letting your mob have a go."

"Don't flatter yourself," he huffed, but she could tell it was a front. A feeble one at that. Jimmy offered a shrug. "And it never actually happened, did it?"

"Intent is everything," she shot back. "And while we're on the topic of my agenda, it happens to be liberating my people from oppression, including slavers like you, and *especially* Nazis."

Jimmy approached the glowing security forcefield, clasping his hands behind his back. "You'll find out, when you've been in the business as long as I have, it's best to pick your battles, me girl."

Sinari felt a rage building in her gut, spreading into her chest like a primal fire. She wondered if this was what her ancestors felt like, preparing for war. But she narrowed her focus, using that fire to feed her words. "I'm not *in the business*, Jimmy. My battle right now is finding and destroying that thermacite lab. And deciding whether you're of any remaining use to me in pursuit of that goal. Because if I decide you're not, I can put in the extradition forms tonight and have your sorry ass on a rocket back to Venus first thing to-morrow."

Sinari held all the cards, and Jimmy knew it. He also knew he had to dig up whatever was left in his charm reserves to extract himself from a predicament that had gone from bad to worse in the matter of a single day.

"I'm pretty sure Rotwald didn't make me. We've done a few deals in the past. If you let me radio in, I might be able to talk him into giving me another shot. After all, he did take our money."

Did he really say 'our money'? Sinari rolled her eyes at the unflappable calm of the man—at least when he wasn't getting shot at. "I'll get you on the radio. And we'll see if we can trian-gulate his signal. Then we go in, get Tana, and bring down their whole operation."

"Ambitious, but not impossible. Especially if you bring some friends."

"Well let's see—we have me, a Terran crim-inal, an ape with multiple university degrees, and an alien robot. Who else did you have in mind?"

Jimmy shook his head, bewildered. "*Tsk tsk,* me girl. Think about it. What about the locals you liberated today? They're an asset. They'll be looking for vengeance, and they owe you a favor. Leverage that."

Leverage that? Sinari grimaced at the thought of leveraging loyalty, especially if it meant putting civilians in harm's way. But he wasn't wrong. She closed her eyes and nodded thoughtfully. "I'll put the word out."

She pressed the button on the wall outside the cell that deactivated the Lenzium field, and walked Jimmy to the radio center, putting a young technician on the signal trace.

Jimmy put in the call to Rotwald's lab, and was finally connected with the scientist. It took some storytelling, but Jimmy explained that he didn't know the parties prior to the exchange. In retrospect, he thought they might even be AEGIS agents. He tried negotiating for Tana under the guise of her being wanted by the Venusian underworld, but that was a dead-end. Rotwald was also unsympathetic to Jimmy's plea for restitution, as the cash was exchanged for goods. That the goods exploded after the deal was done was of no concern to him.

Ultimately, the fact that Jimmy had done a handful of successful deals with Rotwald's operation convinced him to let Jimmy have another shot. He would have to come alone to a checkpoint at the mouth of Long Canyon outside Tempe Terra, and bring an AEGIS tri-crystal engine. In exchange he would be rewarded with enough counterfeit thermacite to fund a lavish retirement.

"That's a new wrinkle," Sinari quipped as Jimmy hung up the radio receiver. "He wants a proprietary tri-crystal engine? To reverse-engineer, I suppose."

"That'd be my guess," Jimmy agreed. "Probably a bit more reliable than their sigil engines."

Sinari had only heard vague rumors of the Reich using a battery of eldritch power, something developed in the late 1920s on Earth by an occult organization called the *Astrum Argentum*. She didn't know the technical details, but apparently when the battery housing was damaged the extradimensional entity trapped inside tended to escape and devour the user—along with anyone in the local vicinity.

Fortunately they were reserved for spacecraft and heavy weaponry, not anything they'd be facing with this particular group of SS troops.

At least, not *likely*.

"But why does he think you can access one?" she wondered aloud.

"Probably because he thinks I'm an AEGIS patsy, and he's planning to give me a raygun welcome wagon. I don't like this. Not one bit." Jimmy leaned forward, rubbing his temples like he had in the cell. "But if I'd said no, we wouldn't have the meet, and you wouldn't have the lab's location."

"Jimmy Two-Fingers," Sinari gasped in faux astonishment. "Are you growing a spine?"

Drake poked his head into the radio room. "Grav sleds are waiting in the vehicle bay. One for Nariaal, and one for Jimmy here."

"And I suppose you've got us in that old Crossley?"

"Oh no. Speed is of the essence. I found us something much faster than the truck."

"Well then," she said, "we'd best get to it."

Drake saluted and began to leave.

"One more thing," Sinari added, halting Drake in mid-stride. "We need a dummy TC engine."

Drake gave a brief look of surprise, but rolled with the news. "I'll get Nariaal on it."

Sinari shook her head, beckoning Drake into the room. "I'll talk to him. I need you here to babysit our friend while he makes a radio call."

Jimmy raised an eyebrow. "So I can let my gang know I'm okay?"

"Not *just* that you're okay," Sinari countered. "AEGIS is offering your whole gang amnesty if they pitch in with the operation. Tell them that."

Jimmy blinked in disbelief. "You're serious?"

Sinari cocked her head at him as she swapped positions with Drake. "I'm serious. You bring your gang and their guns, you all get off the hook. If we can get Tana out safely, I might even throw in hazard pay. That's how badly I want Rotwald."

"I'll tell them," Jimmy said with a smile.

Sinari paused by the radio room door. "You've got five minutes." Then she was gone.

CHAPTER 15

Tana woke to find herself strapped to some kind of metal chair, similar to one that might be found in a dentist's office on Earth—not that she'd ever experienced one in that context. As her vision unclouded, she began to take in her surroundings. The room was windowless, carved out of canyon rock, with the same hues of reds and browns in horizontal strata. It wasn't spacious to begin with, and was made even more cramped by the placement of various technical gadgets and random medical equipment. A metal door at the far corner appeared to be the sole exit.

As torture chambers went, this one was sub-par at best.

Still, she'd been in worse places.

Testing the leather straps holding her wrists and ankles, she realized a direct escape was unlikely. She also noticed she'd been secured palms upward. Her weapons lay on a metal work table on the right side of the room, well out of reach even if she managed to free a limb. She'd just have to wait for an opportunity to present itself, and work from there.

Don't panic, Tana, she thought. *You've dealt with the worst of the Venusian syndicates. These Nazis are worse than that, but you can bear up. You'll just have to be extremely crafty, and completely present.*

She leaned her head back and feigned unconsciousness just as the sound of a bolt sliding echoed through the corridor outside, and the heavy door opened inward. Dr. Rotwald entered in his white lab coat, followed by an assistant of some kind, similarly dressed and carrying a large medical bag.

"And how is our guest doing this evening?" The scientist's voice was calm, his demeanor casual.

Tana gave a small groan and opened her eyes in a groggy flutter. "Do you strap all your guests to industrial furniture?"

"No," Rotwald chuckled. "Just AEGIS agents."

Tana considered denial as a tactic, but realized saying, 'AEGIS? What's that?' while wearing a uniform festooned with service patches would just come off as silly.

"So it's the V.I.P. treatment," she sighed. "Well then, the accommodations are completely unsatisfactory, and the service is appalling. I will be filing a complaint."

The assistant placed his medical bag on a small rolling table and maneuvered it beside the exam chair as Rotwald pulled up his own stool.

"I will be sure to share your feedback with hotel management," he quipped, reaching into the bag and producing a small rectangular case.

Tana tracked his movements with suspicion. "You're not gonna get much from me under torture," she warned. "Venusians are highly resistant to physical coercion."

Rotwald gave a look of shocked disappointment. "My dear, I'm not a monster. I detest torture. And as a scientist, I also know information gained under torture is unreliable at best." He opened the case and drew out a metal syringe, screwing a long needle to one end. "I prefer a more direct line to my data."

As she watched, he reached into the case a second time, pulling out a small ampule of

clear fluid, holding it between thumb and forefinger so she could see.

"Sodium thiopental. Still experimental, but
early results are promising. It relaxes the body
and places the subject into a somewhat 'sug-
gestible' mental state, lowering inhibitions and
allowing for a more *truthful* exchange than
would normally be possible."

There it was. This was to be the focus of
her fight. While Tana had never experienced
this particular drug, the Venusian underworld
had a long history of using various "truth
serums" to glean tactical advantage over a
competing gang or faction. Part of a gangster's
initiation into the syndicates was a display of
mental fortitude when it came to being under
the influence of mind-altering chemicals.

This would be a test of her old training. It
could get interesting, to say the least.

Rotwald prepared the syringe with the fluid
while the assistant pushed up Tana's sleeve
and swabbed the inside of her arm with alco-
hol.

The odor hit her nostrils and she flinched,
immediately berating herself for the display of
panic, however brief.

"We're going to have a nice chat, you and I.
And you're going to tell me all the interesting
details about the AEGIS operations on Mars."
The German scientist held the syringe in full

view, thumbing the plunger enough to coax any air bubbles out with a small eruption of liquid from the needle—the same needle that entered her arm with a pinch. There was a strange, silent pause as pressure grew at the injection site, and then Rotwald handed the equipment to the assistant, who packed it away.

Her body flushed and blood surged to her ears, muffling all sound. The pain was gone in mere moments, and Tana's world became a warm, fluffy pillow.

◌

Sinari entered the lab as Nariaal and Zed were on their way out.

"Ah, Lieutenant," the ape scientist growled. "We were just coming to fetch you. I have something to assist the operation. Over here." He beckoned her into the workshop toward the counter that ran along the back of the room.

She followed in Zed's wake, taking notice of a new metal housing which had been added to the alien robot's back. It somewhat resembled a beetle carapace, with a blockier, more industrial shape. Two exhaust ports at the bottom were trimmed in chrome, while the overall paint scheme was AEGIS blue.

"What's with the new hardware, Zed?" she wondered aloud.

The robot came to a halt next to the workbench and turned to address her, its single round eye aglow. "Dr. Nariaal has fitted me with a 'jump pack', to assist in combat maneuvers."

Sinari squinted past the single robot eye to Nariaal, who grabbed an identical pack from the counter and held it up for display. This one had a leather harness that looked like it might fit a humanoid adult across the chest and shoulders.

"I have another two ready, but they're going into standard production soon." Nariaal grinned, a rare glimpse of childlike pride in his work. "They're wired to a trigger mechanism on the knuckle of the left or right index finger, with the cable fed either outside or inside the sleeve—although the latter might be somewhat uncomfortable. They don't provide great altitude, but can give you about ninety meters distance at a go. Unfortunately no sustained flight. Yet."

The room went quiet as Sinari stared at him in disbelief. Casting a sideways glance at Zed, she crossed her arms. "I'm sorry, did you say, 'combat maneuvers'?"

The robot nodded. "Affirmative."

Sinari returned her gaze to Nariaal. "Who said anything about 'combat maneuvers'?"

"You did say 'standard support tasks', and I assumed we could use all the—"

"I wasn't going to use it in the field yet," Sinari snapped. "And now you've got it fitted with a jump pack to aid in... 'combat maneuvers'." She stared at them for several seconds in uncomfortable silence. "What's the top speed?" she finally asked, nodding her head at the apparatus in Nariaal's massive hands.

"Yet to be determined. Our brief field test today gave us roughly one-hundred kilometers per hour, in short jumps. The unit needs to recalibrate its internal gyroscope after each flight, which takes a second or so. Be sure to wear eye protection in the open air. And a helmet wouldn't hurt." He paused, pondering how best to break the bad news. "They're also a bit pricey in terms of resources, as they use both Lenzium and energite crystals. But Colonel Stevenson was happy to do a limited production run specifically for the Space Rangers program."

"That's incredible," was all Sinari could manage. She suddenly found herself extremely worried about bringing the most ingenious mind in AEGIS to a gunfight against Nazi soldiers. "Are you sure you're up for this?" she asked, adding a nod at the robot. "Both of you?"

"Affirmative, Lieutenant," Zed answered in his tinny mechanical voice. "The doctor has programmed me in a variety of support functions which will increase the likelihood of mission success by at least twenty-seven-point-eight-five percent. I have also been fitted with a personal ablative Lenzium forcefield."

"Twenty-seven-point-eight-five... hold on, did you say *forcefield*?" Sinari traded another look with Nariaal, who shrugged.

"I keep busy," said the ape. "Unfortunately I only have the one unit made, and I'm still fine-tuning the design. I presumed it would be most expedient to outfit the member of this team who will likely be the greatest target of fire."

"I am programmed to protect my fellow Space Rangers," Zed added. "And to terminate Nazis with extreme prejudice."

Sinari paused, her head humming with questions like a hive of wasps. She finally settled on the issue of Dr. Nariaal putting himself in the thick of the fight. "But are you *sure* you want to take a combat role—"

Nariaal extended a calloused palm, cutting her off. "I was raised on Sanctuary Island on Earth, among diverse beast folk. The first of our kind were created by a madman who engaged in cruel and unethical experiments on animals. Yet, if not for that cruelty and pain, four generations later, I would not exist."

Sinari bowed her head as if listening to one of her tribal elders speak their clan history.

"We were a pacifist society. Our primary law was not to spill blood. Yet, when evil came to our shores to enslave and abuse us, I took up arms to fight for our freedom—a fight which included humans willing to lay down their own lives for our liberty. Therefore, do not ask whether I would do the same for my friends and allies. My answer, and my will, is absolute."

The ape spoke so eloquently and with such gravitas that Sinari felt her eyes begin to mist with tears. Composing herself as best she could, she nodded resolutely.

"Well then. Nothing more to be said. Bring the jump packs to the garage and let's get underway."

"I never got a chance to thank you for catching Karpis," Jimmy hailed from the driver's seat of the grav sled.

Sinari frowned through the echoing noise of the garage. "Karpis was your guy?"

"He was," Jimmy smiled. "We only found out he'd been skimming shards after he bugged out. You saved me a bullet." He turned his attention to the controls, giving a slight shrug as he powered on the motor. "Anyway, thanks."

Sinari and Drake watched as the sled bearing Jimmy and the dummy engine pulled out of the motor pool into the Martian night. She hadn't connected Karpis with Jimmy at first, but had to admit it made sense.

A few minutes later, Dr. Nariaal departed with Zed at the controls of another grav sled, leaving the two Rangers alone in the cavernous motor pool.

"You think we can trust Jimmy to get in?" Drake wondered aloud.

Sinari shrugged into her jump pack harness and grunted under the weight. "He has nothing to gain and everything to lose if he crosses me, so yes, I think we can trust him." She turned to Drake, their eyes locking—amethyst to sapphire.

It was suddenly very warm in the garage.

"So," she said finally, "what about this surprise transportation you've cooked up?"

"Oh, I didn't do the cooking," he smirked. "But it's a tasty confection indeed."

He nodded toward a transparent causeway which led to one of the smaller rocket landing pads behind the ASA complex, slinging his own pack over his right shoulder.

She followed, wondering what this man had up his sleeve. Surprises weren't her most favorite thing, especially on the eve of a major operation. But he'd earned some trust over the past few days. At the very least, it wouldn't be that uncomfortable bench seat in the Crossley.

They skirted one of the larger platforms as an enormous transport bearing the V-T-C markings of the Venusian Trading Company—ironically a Terran corporation—ascended into the darkening sky, leading a plume of white-hot sparks. They paused momentarily, watching the takeoff from behind the wall of the glass tube. Then Drake gestured ahead, and they continued.

The causeway terminated in what looked like an office waiting room, with a mammoth set of double doors, guarded by two helmeted ASA security personnel. Drake nodded, and they waved the pair through, holding one of the doors open for them.

Sinari's breath caught in her throat as she caught sight of the landing pad. "Light of the Goddess," she whispered.

"Actually, it's the R-22," Drake quipped in reply.

Standing on three retractable legs was a rocket unlike any Sinari had seen before. There were a few similarities where the basics were concerned, but it was otherwise quite unique and forward-thinking. Like many designs, the main body was cylindrical, tapering to a missile point in front. A forward sensor antenna thrust from the nose like a narwhal horn, and the egg-shaped dome of the cockpit sat just forward of the midpoint, locking hatch on top. A sail-like stabilizing fin was placed aft, above the rear hull.

A pair of engines—she assumed tri-crystal configuration—were set on either side of the craft, with a swept wing branching out from each, arching backward. A secondary thrust engine was attached to the outside of each wing, which Sinari gathered were not so much for atmospheric lift as for housing the two heavy ray weapons in each elegant arm.

There were running lights on the wings, above and below, and on the tail fin. The main body was a brushed steel, with everything else painted a semi-metallic red. She could see the Space Rangers unit insignia on the tail fin, and some kind of identifying marks or logo on the wings which she couldn't make out from her current vantage.

"Six months ago, AEGIS had me testing the prototype. I didn't know it was in production until Nariaal clued me in tonight."

Sinari blinked, speechless. The organization was clearly making some big moves when it came to prepping for the conflict everyone assumed was on the horizon. And this was definitely getting added to her unit hardware requisitions.

"R-22, huh?"

Drake saw her look of shock and it made him smile. "It's not the most spacious," he said, "but it'll get us to the canyon quickly."

Once she'd returned her eyes to their sockets, Sinari shook her head in disbelief. "And you know how to fly it?"

"I haven't taken it into space, but atmospheric flight, yeah." The landing bay lights glinted in the corner of his eye. "Like I said, I was a test dummy for this bird."

"But you're not with the Aeronautics division. You're a—"

"Criminal?" Drake finished. "Yeah, they didn't wanna waste good pilots on the test program when blowing up was a risk. Just needed volunteers to put in the seat, but I picked up the controls pretty easily, and made some extra hazard pay as well."

"Gaming the system," Sinari smirked, recalling their first conversation in the truck just days ago.

"When the system exists to keep most down while elevating others..."

"It should be gamed," Sinari said with absolute finality on the topic. "So," she nodded, pointing at the brand-spanking-new ship on the landing pad, "shall we take her out?"

Drake bowed at the waist, extending his arm to point the way. "Lieutenants first."

CHAPTER 16

Jimmy Two-Fingers arrived at the canyon mouth at sunset, with the Martian sky awash in bands of orange and blood red. The twilight air was crisp and cool.

His grav sled had seen better days, pocked with dings and streaked with desert dust. The original color might have been a bright gold, but between the wear and faded paint, it now resembled a slab of mottled sandstone. It was just under five meters long and half that wide, with an engine compartment in the front, protected by a transparent half-dome of acrylic plastic. Three padded seats were set behind the curved windscreen—one in the center at the flight controls, and two aft of the pilot's chair. The rest of the vehicle was a flat, open bed which hovered on a Lenzium repulsor field.

He wore his long leather coat and hooded mantle, goggles, and dust gaiter. Behind him, in the cargo area, sat an object the size of a tractor's engine block, draped with a canvas tarpaulin. Dr. Nariaal had cobbled together a power pack wired to a large container of lab-grown thermacite and contained in a tri-crystal engine housing. Impressively, he'd done it in the vehicle garage in about four minutes flat just before they departed. It was essentially a jury rigged explosive device which would incinerate everyone in a ten-meter radius when switched on.

The sentries waved him to a halt, and he slowed his approach. One of the soldiers straddled a Horex motorcycle with an empty sidecar—some sort of messenger or runner, Jimmy presumed. Another approached the sled with a ray carbine at the ready. The third hopped up in the back to inspect the object under the tarp. A few seconds was all it took, and the third soldier leaped down from the open bed and signaled the second trooper, who waved Jimmy through. With the motorcycle leading the way, Jimmy slowly negotiated the half-kilometer of canyon until they arrived at the loading bay.

Carved from desert rock, the open mouth of the vehicle depot stretched a hundred and fifty meters wide and over fifteen meters high, hinting at a much more cavernous space within. The motorcycle escort led Jimmy into the massive facility, where a small army of laborers—mostly Red Martians and Venusian Gan—trudged back and forth, stacking crates of lab-grown crystals, loading them into trucks or larger storage containers which were ferried away to parts unknown.

As Jimmy slowed his grav sled to a halt in the designated space, he estimated how much explosive volatility was being moved around in this one space, and how absolutely no one would survive if it were all to go up at once.

CR

Tana's head lolled forward, a thin line of drool descending from her lower lip. She breathed slowly, quietly, with a slight wheeze brought on by the constriction of her airway as her chin hit her chest. Blood surged to her face, swelling her scarred cheek like a strawberry painted gold.

Keep your head, girl, she thought. *Don't let yourself fall into the darkness.*

The assistant tilted her head back against the rest, securing it with a strap. As he did so, he gently pried open her eyes and checked her pupil dilation. "She's ready," he announced.

"Good," answered the doctor, leaning forward in the metal office chair. "Now, Tana, I'm going to ask you a series of questions..."

Tana's inner monologue echoed through a seemingly cavernous void. *Ask all the questions you want, Nazi scum. I will resist you with every fiber of my being.*

As Rotwald opened his mouth to speak the next words, there was a sharp knock from the hall. He gave an exasperated nod to the assistant, who went to the door and pulled it open.

Another white-smocked scientist stepped excitedly into the room.

"What is it?" Rotwald demanded.

The younger scientist handed a single sheet of paper to the assistant, rambling excitedly in German. "You wanted to be notified when the new variant of thermacite crystal was ready. We have reached an entirely new level of volatility."

Rotwald let out a heavy grunt of exasperation. "That is excellent news, doctor, but as you can see, I'm conducting an interrogation. You may return to your work. I will visit you in the lab later."

The young scientist clicked his boot heels together and offered a Nazi salute. *"Heil Hitler!"* he announced before turning back toward the lab.

Rotwald sighed as the assistant shut the door and handed him the report. Almost instantly, another knock sounded from outside.

"What the Devil—?!" This time, Rotwald stormed to the door himself, flinging it open to find a uniformed soldier in desert fatigues standing at attention.

"Herr Doktor!" the soldier addressed formally. "You wanted to be informed when the Venusian had arrived at the loading dock."

The report crumpled in his clenched fist, yet he managed an otherwise calm outward demeanor. "Thank you. Please tell the duty officer I shall arrive presently."

Another extended arm salute, and the trooper disappeared down the hall.

Rotwald cast a look of mock pity at Tana as she sat, strapped semiconscious to the interrogation chair. "Alas, my dear, our conversation must be delayed for a few minutes, as I need to finish some business with your countryman. This shan't take long." He handed the report back to the assistant, regarding him closely. "Stay here with her. Turn on the wire recorder, make note of anything she says."

The assistant saluted, but Rotwald was already out the door.

ॐ

The open desert streaked by in a dark orange blur, tinged with the gunmetal blue of the approaching night. Drake Dawson gripped the flight yoke of the rocket, guiding it silently toward their objective. Specifically, *he* was silent. The rocket made a noise like an angry swarm of wasps, tri-crystal engines throwing off a cascade of golden sparks into the rapidly darkening sky. They were conspicuous to say the least. There was just no way to be stealthy in one of these things.

But with Jimmy already on site, they could use the weaponry on the rocket to create quite the diversion, allowing for the second part of the plan to occur.

"What's the second part again?" Drake tilted his head toward Sinari.

Leaning over the right side of the pilot's chair, she gazed out through the forward viewport. "Jimmy brings the dummy engine to Rotwald. If they fire it up in the loading bay, kaboom. If they take it out into the canyon, smaller kaboom. He's buying time for us to get on the ground there."

A shape whizzed by under the rocket.

"We just passed Nariaal's sled," Drake observed.

Sinari pursed her lips in thought. "They'll catch up," she said. "We have to park this thing out of sight and use the packs to make our entry."

Drake was stunned. "You mean we're not using the rocket to shoot our way in?"

"Not with Jimmy and an unknown number of local laborers already in the facility. And Tana."

"Well that's disappointing," Drake sighed.

"I'll grant that it would be fun to use the goodies on this thing to blast our way in," Sinari laughed, giving Drake's shoulder a friendly squeeze, "but it's overkill in this instance." She patted that same shoulder, wondering who this strange woman was—the woman who exuded supreme confidence on the surface while her insides churned with the reality of the situation. There were far too many variables at play, too many moving parts to have a semblance of real confidence in any of it.

She decided her plan was haphazard at best, and the lives of her fellow Rangers—not to mention countless civilians—were on the line. Not an auspicious start to her command. She could only hope that Rotwald would grossly overestimate her reaction to the botched transaction in the desert. If nothing else, his methodical mind might not be expecting the chaos they were about to bring to his doorstep.

"Coming up on the Long Canyon," Drake announced.

Sinari nodded affirmation. "Bring us around to the north exit. We'll use the jump packs from there." She wrinkled her nose, throwing a glance at the jump packs secured to the bottom of the ladder which led to the top hatch. "I don't know about you, but I'm gonna need some practice with these things."

◌

Jimmy casually scanned the loading bay interior, while reaching under the dashboard controls and popping one of the ignition cables loose without attracting anyone's attention. He was especially nervous being in such close proximity to the soldier who'd ridden escort and was now dismounting the motorcycle. The soldier turned, un-shouldering his carbine and keeping it trained vaguely in Jimmy's direction. Their eyes met briefly, and Jimmy turned his attention back to the depot.

The place had to have been a Red Martian outpost at some point—the stonework was too old and too precise to have been constructed since the Nazis' arrival. Some of the walls were etched in reliefs depicting pivotal moments in Barsoom history, and the arched corridors spreading outward beneath the mountains carried an archaic, native motif. The enormous depot was lit by a grid of hanging incandescent lamps and functioned as half motor pool, half warehouse.

Pairs of soldiers watched the loading of vehicles from atop metal catwalks, with a few scattered among the Martian workers on the floor. He counted twelve in all, and twenty unarmed Red warriors. The laborers threw the occasional glance his way, but he did his best to avoid direct eye contact.

He wasn't worried about having to fight Red Martians—they would most likely turn against the soldiers if given the right opportunity, or flee to the mountains outside. The dozen Waffen-SS troops armed with those ray carbines gave him more pause. This was not an open air environment. They'd have a much better chance of picking him off here in an enclosed space, especially from the catwalks above. Jimmy recalled an Earth saying about "shooting fish in a barrel", which made no sense to him, but was supposed to reference something being particularly easy. Regardless of how stupid he found the analogy, he had no desire to be said fish in said barrel. On the other hand, there was plenty of cover and, with enough Martians in revolt, and enough chaos...

But bringing the chaos was not his part of the operation. He was merely here to get the dummy TC engine inside the bay. His present concerns were the armed soldiers and a couple dozen crates of explosive artificial thermacite packed into the space. He would not be the one to fire the first shot. He would sit in the driver's seat of the grav sled and wait.

And he didn't have to wait for long. Not five minutes after parking in the loading bay, Rotwald appeared in the easternmost archway, flanked by two soldiers. He was in full uniform, including officer's cap and long coat, and appeared to be wearing some kind of additional harness of brown leather underneath it.

"Jimmy," he hailed. "So good of you to make the trip out here a second time."

The Venusian gangster offered a casual salute and stood from the pilot's seat. "I take my business quite seriously, *Herr Doktor.*" He turned to the open bed and pulled the tarp from the dummy engine, gesturing at it. "As you can see, I have upheld my end of the deal. A new tri-crystal engine, direct from the south landing pad at Mars 1. It's pristine, and was not an easy score. Fortunately, I have some sticky fingers working for me at the ASA docks."

Rotwald strode to the edge of a raised area at the back of the loading bay and leaned forward on the iron railing. The engine was roughly the same size and shape as two steamer trunks stacked atop one another, a streamlined case containing a multitude of high-voltage wires and three distinct crystal reaction chambers. "I can believe that," he said, watching as the two soldiers descended a short stairwell of concrete and moved toward the grav sled, weapons at the ready.

Jimmy felt a knot of panic swell in his gut, and he knew somehow Rotwald could tell.

"Or, I would believe it," the doctor continued, "if I didn't already know you to be an AEGIS asset." He nodded to the soldiers, who beckoned Jimmy down from the back of the sled. "My dance card has become somewhat full today, so you will do me the courtesy of waiting in my office while I attend to some pressing business. If the tri-crystal engine you brought is the genuine article, I may let you live, and employ you as an AEGIS informant. If it's a fake, as I suspect it is, it will be my pleasure to blast a hole through your alien brain." He made a gun with his thumb and forefinger, miming a shot.

That was unnecessary, Jimmy thought. He'd never liked Rotwald, per se. But now he could accurately say he hated him. "I don't work for AEGIS," he protested. I didn't know those were agents—they cleared our background check—"

Rotwald held up a hand to stop him. *"Bringen Sie die Maschine aus der Anlage und prüfen Sie, ob sie funktioniert,"* he ordered the soldiers. One of the pair leaped into the bed of the vehicle and nudged him onto the ground, where the other soldier held him at gunpoint. The Martian laborers continued stealing glances, but dared not pause their work.

Jimmy turned to look out through the wide exit, his brain counting steps to at least four different sources of decent cover. Then the soldier in the grav sled sat in the pilot's chair and tried powering on, and Jimmy broke out in a nervous sweat.

The vehicle sat unmoving. The dynamo that powered its repulsor field still whirred away, but the instrument panel remained dark, no forward or reverse thrust available. He clicked the ignition switch three more times, with no effect.

The soldier looked up at Rotwald, whose face wrinkled with suspicion.

Jimmy heard the electric zap of rayguns in the canyon outside, and two figures suddenly appeared, blue streaks leaping through the air at great speed.

Rotwald's own laser sidearm was in his hand instantly.

Sinari landed on the roof of one of the cargo trucks parked against the north wall, raygun trained on Rotwald himself. Drake bounded up a stack of wooden crates on the south side, lighting on the main catwalk. He grabbed a guard in a choke hold, jamming his pistol into the soldier's kidney as he whirled the bulky jump pack against the man's partner. The second soldier screamed as he plunged headfirst onto the concrete floor below with a gruesome *spack!*

"Nobody move!" Sinari ordered, tracking her pistol across the loading bay.

The Red Martian laborers immediately stopped working and began hunting around for tools or anything that could be used as a weapon. Jimmy grabbed the soldier's gun from the ground, edging away from the grav sled and the potential bomb in the back.

Sinari and Drake exchanged a nod. They'd made it inside. It was more than she imagined they might accomplish. Drake gave her a charming wink, which made her stomach flutter despite the situational tension.

"Dr. Rotwald," she said. "You are in violation of interplanetary and Martian law. Order your men to stand down and surrender the premises, or we will use lethal force."

As if to illustrate, the soldier guarding Jimmy raised his carbine, and Sinari drilled a smoldering hole in his chest with a beam of crackling red light. She turned back to Rotwald, cocking her head.

"Your call, *Doktor.*"

Rotwald sighed, thumbing some kind of toggle switch on the belt harness, and a shimmering blue energy field seemed to swallow him up.

Sinari glanced at Drake on the hanging gantry. "Forcefield!" she alerted.

"Bloody hell," Drake grunted, shoving his pistol into his captive's back with gusto as he leaned over for a better vantage. It was only then that he—and Sinari—realized the doctor's exit plan.

Smiling, the Nazi scientist lowered his pistol at the cargo bed of Jimmy's vehicle, and fired.

CHAPTER 17

"Take cover!" Dawson cried as the grav sled erupted in billowing flame, sending a random assortment of industrial bolts and aluminum shards rocketing out in all directions. He felt a series of stings pepper across his left arm—the only part of him exposed by holding the Nazi soldier across the neck—and felt his hostage drop limply.

The shockwave was brief, but searing hot.

Miraculously, the domed windscreen in the grav sled contained the brunt of the forward explosion, keeping it from igniting the stacked crates on the loading dock, although the soldier in the pilot's seat wasn't so fortunate. His scream was cut short as he was consumed by the fireball. The force of the blast punched a hole in the cargo bed and rattled the brackets suspending the catwalk from the walls and ceiling. Repulsor emitters sputtered and failed, and the grav sled slammed to the ground.

Jimmy poked his head from behind a wall of oil drums near the depo's wide entry, taking aim at the closest targets he could find, dropping one soldier, then another. He'd been yanked around once too often by these thugs, who used violence to control those weaker than them. They stole his business model, and that would not stand.

Sinari found herself launched against the wall in front of the cargo truck's front grille, ears ringing, head swimming. She staggered upright, using the jump pack against the wall for leverage. Pushing her goggles onto her forehead, she scanned through the fire and smoke for Rotwald, but couldn't see him.

An alarm bell sounded, loud and constant. The clanging mixed with the screams of wounded soldiers and Martian laborers sprawled burned and bleeding on the depot floor.

"Dawson!" Sinari hailed. "Do you see him?"

"Negative!" came the reply from above, followed by the *crunch* of the hostage soldier hitting the loading bay. Sweeping his view across the interior, Drake located the rapidly clanging alarm bell set high into the north wall. His pistol lit up red as he took aim, heating to amber as he pulled the trigger. The alarm became a melted streak of metal in a flash of hot crimson energy. At least it was a great deal quieter in the room.

The surviving Martians were already scavenging whatever undamaged weapons they could from the wounded SS, but Sinari knew fresh troops would soon be flooding the loading bay. They had to act quickly.

Damnit, where's Nariaal?

The appearance of an unfamiliar troop truck at the depot's canyon entrance drew Sinari's attention. Jimmy, standing combat--ready behind his oil drums, was suddenly flanked by a dozen gangsters—mostly Terrans and Venusian Gan like himself. They carried Tommy guns and ray pistols, and looked ready for a fight.

"Good to see ya, Boss," hailed a short fireplug of an Italian with hairy knuckles and a leather flight jacket. He clutched the grip of his Tommy gun with effortless control. "You want we should get rid of the Bluesuits?"

Jimmy knew he was referring to Sinari and Drake, in their navy blue uniforms. He wondered if this was his opportunity to wriggle off the hook and escape. However, there was always a chance the Nazis would track him down and deal with him in their own inimitable, brutal fashion. He wasn't overly fond of that possibility existing.

"Jimmy," Sinari hailed from the front of the cargo truck, extending her pistol in his direction. "What are you doing?"

Drake used the jump pack to leap safely onto the hood of the cargo truck, raygun trained on the short gangster.

Jimmy dropped the Nazi carbine to his side and put up his left hand. "Nothing, Vohn."

"What are ya talking about, Boss?" the gangster lieutenant quipped. "We got a baker's dozen, and there's just two of them. We got 'em, easy."

A symphony of submachine gun bolts ratcheting back echoed through the hall, followed by the electronic whine of ten ray weapons powering up. Jimmy's gangsters were suddenly faced with a group of angry Martians and their scavenged Nazi carbines. At the same moment, a collection of Martians Sinari had liberated after the desert firefight arrived at the depot entrance, armed to the teeth with rayguns and native weapons.

Gangsters and Red Martians stood in tense silence, looks exchanged and weapons aimed at each other around the depot floor. Sinari and Drake braced themselves for a fight.

"Jimmy…" Sinari repeated. "What's it going to be?"

The standoff only lasted moments before the sound of boots at double-time reached their ears from the interior corridors.

Jimmy clamped his free hand on his lieutenant's shoulder. "No Lou. The Bluesuits aren't the enemy—at least not today. We got us a marriage of convenience. *Capisce?*"

The lieutenant relaxed his weapon, and the other gangsters followed suit. "So what's the play?"

Jimmy gave Sinari a nod that conveyed a promise of alliance… for now. "The play," he answered, "is them." Raising the energy carbine toward the depot's centermost hallway, he waited for the troops to arrive. The rag-tag assortment of criminals, liberated workers, and two increasingly nervous Space Rangers turned with weapons ready.

The loading dock was suddenly full of Waffen-SS troopers, blasting away with their ray-guns, almost immediately igniting the stacked crates of illicit thermacite. The chain reaction from crate to crate filled the depot with shards of wood and fragments of sizzling crystal. Several Martian laborers and a handful of Jimmy's gangsters were ripped to shreds in an instant.

Shrapnel zipped like razor blades, slicing jagged shreds in the arms and legs of Sinari's canvas uniform as she covered her face and torso, curling into a ball behind the truck bonnet. The concussion launched Drake from the hood, but moments before he collided with the north wall, he hit the thrust on the jump pack, reducing the impact to a few bruised ribs instead of broken ones.

Just as Sinari righted herself and was about to get her rag-tag army to fall back, another grav sled burst into the depot, alien robot Zed at the controls, Dr. Nariaal clutching a chrome raygun in each mighty ape fist. The sled rushed in at speed, skidding on air parallel to the loading dock—which was now a sizzling mess of melted metal and crystalline slag. Nariaal picked off Nazi soldiers one at a time, in rapid succession, as the first rank was replenished from the corridor behind them.

The mob inside the vehicle bay surged forward, weapons blazing. The loading dock became a cat's cradle of zig-zagging laser beams.

Sinari struggled to her feet and thumbed the jump pack control on her left index finger to launch herself onto the loading platform, firing the chrome raygun in her right hand. She landed, noting pain in her right knee and looking down to see the leg of her uniform torn in several places and a shard of jagged crystal protruding from the joint a couple of centimeters. Reaching down with her left hand, she clenched her teeth and pulled the crystal flechette free just as Zed leaped from the pilot's station and strode mechanically through the dying fire. The next group of soldiers were already piling through the interior doorway. The hazy blue orb surrounding Zed shimmered and hummed with every laser blast that came his way, and Sinari decided personal shields would be priority gear for their next mission.

As she watched the robot take point, its large, stage-light eye began to glow—first a deep red, then orange, cycling through yellow to white, finally erupting with a blinding blast of coruscating energy. It cut through the line of Nazi troops, leaving a smoldering black scar across the far wall, and sizzling bodies on the floor.

Sinari caught the simian scientist's eye as he leaped from the grav sled onto the concrete dock.

"I thought you said it wasn't a weapon!"

Nariaal shrugged in his own inimitable way. "I found a subsystem I hadn't seen before."

"When? When did you have time?"

"I was tinkering on the trip out here."

"You were *tinkering*. With your *pilot*. While it was *piloting. The vehicle you were riding in.*"

Nariaal shrugged again, hefting the spare 44-RCX carbine from the bed of the newly-arrived sled and tossing it to Drake. "I wasn't interfering with his piloting routine."

Lt. Dawson caught the weapon and floated to a landing on the edge of the dock, kicking away a pile of crackling debris. Pushing his goggles to his forehead, he ran a gloved hand through a sweaty mass of hair. "Cheers."

Nariaal wasn't finished. "Remember, science is the process of—"

"—seeking answers in an unknown universe," Sinari and Drake finished in unison.

The ape smiled, gratified when the wisdom he conferred took root in the student.

Martians and mobsters were already making their way up the concrete steps toward the inside corridors. Sinari didn't have the time or energy to interrogate Nariaal about his operational priorities. She waved the temporarily-allied parties through, barking, "Secure the facility! Don't kill *everyone*—try to take a few prisoners!" Not that she believed anyone would actually abide by her orders.

"What now, Boss?" Drake asked, keeping a watchful eye on the hallway as the four Space Rangers edged toward the archway among the throng.

"You and Nariaal go find Tana, get her clear," she ordered. "Zed and I are going after Rotwald."

The robot's head jerked back in apparent surprise. "We are?"

"We are," Sinari answered without hesitation. She gestured politely. "And you're walking in front. Rendezvous here, or at the south end of the canyon."

"See you on the other side," Drake saluted, powering on the laser carbine with a high--pitched ascending whine. "Come on, Doctor."

Drake and Nariaal exited eastward, while Sinari and Zed found their way north, toward the lab. Sounds of laser blasts and gunfire called out from the labyrinth of corridors within the facility, merged with the screams of the dying.

CHAPTER 18

The corridor leading eastward was less than three meters wide, allowing for two average-sized humanoids to comfortably pass side-by-side. Or a single humanoid and the massive simian companion behind him. Fortunately, that also meant that any enemy troops Drake and Nariaal encountered would only be two, maybe three abreast. Of course, that number could theoretically double if the front rank knelt to a firing position, but those tactics were surely outdated, weren't they? Napoleonic-era, surely...

Odds were Tana was in one of the medical exam rooms, and Drake did his best to silently translate the German signage at every hallway intersection.

They padded through the labyrinthine corridor in silence, listening for activity ahead. Drake clutched the carbine tightly, left hand on the forward grip, right hand on the pistol grip. The transparent coils surrounding the barrel pulsed an eerie red. "Oi, Doc," he said, remembering the lab demonstration a couple of days previous, with the melted raygun and room full of smoke. "The crystals in our weapons—"

"Are authentic, mined thermacite," Nariaal finished. "Worry not, Ensign."

Drake shrugged, nonchalant in the extreme. "I'm not worried," he insisted. "Who's worried? Not me."

The corridor they traveled continued forward for another thirty meters before coming to a T, but a spur opened to their right just a few paces ahead. A small squad of Jimmy's thugs passed the T section, and the end of the hall lit up with the call and response of red-amber beams of light. Drake and Nariaal headed for the spur, ducking out of sight just as four SS troopers pushed past the gangsters they'd just mowed down.

Instinctively, Drake opened fire at their backs, sweeping across the rear two with a blast from the carbine. The two who had been in front turned with the screams of the troopers behind them, returning fire with their own rayguns. Drake grunted in pain as his left shoulder was opened by an enemy shot and was immediately cauterized with the heat.

Nariaal fired both sidearms from the waist, mowing down the remaining troopers in a salvo of energy blasts.

The ape turned, holstering his pistols to free his massive hands. He spun Dawson toward him and began to examine his shoulder. "Are you badly hurt?"

Drake winced with the probing. "Later," he protested, pulling away. "We have to find Tana."

As the duo passed through a shadow into the light at the end of the spur, they found themselves face to face with three armed SS troops guarding a medical office door. The soldiers were already firing before Drake and Nariaal could fully process their predicament.

Nariaal howled as a searing hot beam of light carved a canal along his right thigh. Drake caught a similar wound down his left bicep, close to the earlier wound.

Gritting his teeth, he dropped to one knee and lit up the carbine at the centermost Nazi soldier, while Nariaal fired his twin pistols at the outside two. All three targets fell where they stood, smoke tendrils reaching dramatically toward the ceiling from smoldering chest wounds.

Drake winced at the pain in his throbbing left arm as he stared at the door. The chances of Tana being left unattended were slim to none. There was almost sure to be someone inside the room with her, armed and ready for target practice the moment they entered. It gave him an idea.

In fact, Drake was correct in his assumption. The lab assistant was ready for them. Armed with a Luger pistol, the young man took up position in the corner of the examination room with a clear line of sight to the locked door. He wasn't sure if the aggressors were disgruntled Martian laborers or AEGIS agents come to rescue one of their own, and he didn't much care. Perspiration collecting on his face made his round spectacles slip down on his nose. He pushed them back up with a nervous finger, pistol quaking in his outstretched right hand.

The high-pitched electric whine of a ray weapon erupted from the hallway outside, and the door handle heated to a white-orange hue before falling to the floor. Then the door flew open, kicked inward by a mighty simian foot. The assistant wasn't sure what he was expecting to come through the open doorway, but odds were against a hulking gorilla in a blue jumpsuit hefting the corpse of an SS trooper as a meat-shield.

Nariaal stepped into the room, found his bespectacled target, and heaved the dead soldier as he would throw out the opening pitch at a baseball game. Before the assistant could fire a single shot, he was flattened against the back wall of the room, tangled in dead limbs and sundry furniture.

Drake was inside immediately, casting a quick look outside to make sure no one was right behind them. Tossing the ray carbine to the counter top, he moved to the side of the exam chair Tana was strapped to.

"Wow," she marveled, head still swimming with the narcotic in her system. "You boys know how to make an entrance."

Drake cracked a smile as he undid the leather straps at her arms and legs. "A command performance. All for you, luv."

'All for you, luv.' Tana paused. She knew that in British culture, the term "love" was used most often as a casual term of endearment. But coming from Ensign Dawson, it meant something more, somehow. Or maybe it was just the drugs.

Yes, it was probably the drugs.

But was it really?

Come on, Tana, she thought. *What are you doing? Get yourself together.*

With Nariaal on her left hand and Drake on her right, Tana rose to a slightly wobbly standing position. Her blue uniform was scuffed with red desert soil, the right sleeve rolled up to the elbow. She'd definitely been injected with something.

The simian scientist looked into her eyes as he performed a rudimentary exam. "Pupils are dilated," he growled. "Do you know what they gave you?"

Tana frowned in thought. "Sodium... theo. Theo something."

Nariaal nodded at Drake. "Sodium thiopental. She'll be alright in a few hours."

Tana waved a casual hand. "I'll be alright in a few hours," she repeated, suddenly spying the ray carbine on the counter. "Ooh! You brought me a gun!"

Drake chuckled under his breath. "Uh, yeah. But I'm gonna carry it for you until we get back to the sled. Okay?"

Tana leaned in close, head in the hollow of his neck. "That's so thoughtful," she breathed, inhaling the scent of sweat and burnt canvas. Then she realized it was the heat wound in his arm causing that particular odor. "Oh no! You're hurt!"

"I'm fine," Drake protested. "Come on, Doc. Let's get out of here."

Clutching Tana on either side, the trio staggered to the doorway. As they passed the tangle of lab assistant and dead Nazi trooper in the corner, the pile of limbs and furniture debris began to shift. Drawing a sidearm from his left holster, Nariaal fired a stream of crimson heat into the assistant's chest, and the pile stopped moving.

Drake grabbed the carbine by its pistol grip and pulled it from the counter top as they exited through the door like some kind of six-legged mutant.

❧

"What you did back there," Sinari began as she and Zed made their way toward the lab facility at the center of the complex. "Can you do that again, on command?"

"Unknown. Please stand by." The robot's gears and circuits whirred and clicked. After a few seconds, the large canister head tilted as if in conversation. "My onboard defense system utilizes an approximation of what you call 'tri-crystal' technology, combining energite, Lenzium, and thermacite in the reaction chamber. According to my internal diagnostic, there is an eighty-seven percent chance that I have one more energy dispersal of that type, before one or more crystals fracture, causing failure of the weapon."

Sinari's brow furrowed, and she gave a heavy sigh. "Well, that's not ideal." She moved forward to the next corner, wincing in pain with every step.

Zed followed, clacking metal feet on the stone floor. "Agreed. Clearly my designers envisioned the weapon as a sort of 'last ditch' feature."

Several white-coated laboratory workers were bustling in and out of a set of double doors at the end of the hall. The signage on the surrounding walls—although Sinari couldn't perfectly translate the German—gave her an indication that this was an important and forbidden area. Several bodies lay strewn about the floors and slumped against walls near the entry, telling her the Martian rebels and a couple of Jimmy's gang had already attempted to get in, unsuccessfully.

"Try to save that shot if you can," she instructed Zed. "Use it on Rotwald."

The robot's head cocked again. "Query: do you no longer wish to take Dr. Rotwald alive?"

"He's not interested in surrender," she answered. "He's made his choice." She looked into Zed's big, translucent eye and found her own reflection staring back. "We're taking him out. Do you have a problem with that?"

"I am programmed to dispatch Nazis—"

"With extreme prejudice," She recalled, throwing a final cautionary look down the twenty meters of corridor to the doors to the lab. Checking her sidearm, she noted the battery charge was active. "Then let's dispatch."

"Affirmative, Lieutenant," Zed nodded, taking point as they advanced toward the laboratory.

As they closed the last ten meters, they surprised a small group of SS leaving the lab, weapons at the ready. Sinari fired over Zed's shoulder, dropping the first. The remaining three opened fire with their energy carbines, lighting up the corridor with scarlet beams of searing light. Zed's shield flashed blue with each hit, as he moved directly to the center-most soldier.

As he closed with the trio, they ceased fire long enough to adjust their firearms to close combat bludgeons.

The robot's arm raised a clenched fist, and in an impossibly quick jackhammer motion, made three upward punches, smashing three jaws, and sending the soldiers rocketing backward against the stone wall, smashing limbs and skulls and spines.

That was a neat trick, Sinari thought, brandishing her chrome raygun as they entered through the double doors.

The thermacite manufacturing laboratory was as spacious as the vehicle bay, partitioned into various workstations by stone half-walls. At the rear of the room stood a row of massive transparent vats in which bubbling fluid grew stalks of ruby-colored crystal. A small number of laboratory workers in white smocks hastily packed various plans and supplies into canvas satchels in order to make their escape.

Standing at the center, surrounded by open bins of red glass-like shards, was Dr. Rotwald. He wore dark-tinted goggles over his eyes and a maniacal grin on his face. Gripping the raygun in his right hand, he raised a small electronic device in his left. He watched, granite-faced, flushed with incendiary rage as the robot entered, followed by Sinari.

"Stop where you are!" he bellowed in English. The lab assistants froze, turning silently to watch the confrontation.

Sinari stood defiantly behind Zed, a clear line of sight over his shoulder. Her pistol was aimed at his chest. "If you won't come peacefully, Doctor, you give us no choice—"

"You give *me* no choice, Lieutenant! The detonator in my hand is set to trigger every last shard of artificial thermacite in this room! You and your robot companion will be consumed."

Rotwald's eyes swelled in their sockets and a small vein throbbed at his left temple. Sinari could tell he was either high on amphetamine or had succumbed to madness—in either case, he was serious. He was really going to do this.

"What about you, Rotwald?" she asked. "You ready to kill your workers, to die yourself?" *What am I saying?* she thought. *Of course he's ready to sacrifice everyone in this place. Stupid question.*

The German scientist offered a smirk of supreme arrogance. "Fortunately I'm equipped with a personal Lenzium forcefield, which should protect me from the blast."

The lab workers traded looks of shock and betrayal.

Sinari breathed slowly. He hadn't seen Zed's forcefield. Of course neither of them knew how much ablative value remained—in either generator. "*Should,* huh? Well we might just have a few surprises up our sleeve as well."

Sinari matched Rotwald's smile, grinning through her pain. "Now, Zed," she whispered, and the robot's head zeroed in on the Nazi scientist.

There was a small *pop* and a puff of smoke, and the eye went dim.

"I'm afraid," Zed muttered softly, "that my optical weapon is no longer functional."

Sinari's heart sank into her stomach, and her eyes grew wide as she watched Rotwald slide his thumb to the detonator. "Oh no."

"Duck," came Zed's appeal in that soft electronic voice.

And the room exploded.

A firestorm of superheated glass shards, bits of rock, and metal debris roared from the center of the room, shredding and incinerating the remaining scientists and lab assistants. Zed and Rotwald stood in place, sensing the force of the blast from behind their respective shimmering blue shields, but suffering none of the destructive effects. Sinari dropped prone and gasped as the air was sucked from her lungs and her body was drummed by the thunderous concussion. At least from her flat position behind Zed, she wasn't riddled with a thousand bits of molten crystal.

The torrent of consuming flame receded as quickly as it had come, leaving behind sizzling fragments of debris and a cloud of smoky haze. The line of transparent vats along the wall had shattered completely, as well as the growing stalks of crystal with them. Several piles of charred skeletons and smoldering clothing were all that remained of the lab personnel.

Sinari gagged, spitting a wad of toxic phlegm to the floor as she rose, shaking, to her knees, scanning through the smoke to find Rotwald. Finally, she found the arrogant silhouette with the field cap and lab coat.

"Lieutenant, the blast has depleted my forcefield," Zed informed her as a heat ray beam came zipping out of the smoke and caught the robot in the chest. The sound of gears and circuits frying merged with the smell of roasting metal, and Sinari stifled an anguished cry.

"Zed!" she whimpered.

Dr. Rotwald strode out of the haze, raygun at the ready.

Glancing in his direction, Sinari watched a tiny rock fragment fall from the ceiling and ricochet off his right shoulder. Then she noted a small cascade of blue sparks at his hip, where he'd originally powered on his Lenzium field. In that moment she realized—

His shield is down too!

Her entire body tensed in a subconscious effort to overcome its tremors. Before she knew it, her finger was squeezing the trigger of her silver raygun, streaming a hot beam of death at Rotwald. It traced up his torso, opening him from belly to neck, leaving a gaping canyon of blackened, cauterized flesh. He screamed but it was cut short by the fountain of blood gushing from his mouth. The scientist swayed on unsteady legs as the realization of his own mortality crushed in on him and he crumpled in place, slamming his knees onto the stone floor.

In a final, desperate act, he raised his pistol toward Sinari, and she fired again, carving a tunnel of red heat through his left eye and out the back of his skull. His body fell forward, face-down on the warm stone floor, a single finger of smoke pointing skyward.

"Hooray for us," Sinari sighed aloud as the darkness closed in on the periphery of her vision, and she prepared to collapse unceremoniously at the robot's side.

No, Vohn, too much yet to do, she thought. *You can sleep later.* She forced the black haze from her field of view and rose—she hadn't a clue as to where she'd been storing the necessary energy—until she stood shakily, a primal act of sheer will and adrenaline.

She had to see Rotwald's body up close, if only to verify that it no longer posed a threat to her, her team, her people, and the very fabric of civil society.

If she had to kick the body a few times to make sure, so much the better.

CHAPTER 19

Jimmy, his right hand Lou, and two of the gang's enforcers worked their way through the labyrinth of Nazi facilities, clearing the corridors of Waffen-SS troops and support personnel. Despite Sinari's directive to spare a few Nazis for further interrogation, Jimmy decided they'd overstayed their welcome and were just gumming up his business. Hence every soldier sighted was a soldier burned down.

They moved from the barracks to the commissary, losing the enforcers to raygun fire one by one along the way. Then Lou and Jimmy swept from the showers to the armory, the latter of which they helped themselves to in a liberal fashion. At least as much as two individuals could carry in a single trip.

At last they found Nariaal and Drake carrying Tana back to the vehicle depot, and they took point for the last several meters. By that time, however, there were no enemies left to target.

Dr. Nariaal spent a few minutes tending Drake's wounds as well as his own, and offered Tana a canteen of water from the pilot's compartment of the grav sled. Drake stayed with Tana in the bed of the vehicle while the ape scientist enlisted Jimmy to accompany him back inside the complex to look for Sinari and Zed.

The remaining gangsters and Martian tribesfolk were already beginning to filter out to the vehicles they arrived in, or on foot into the canyon. Jimmy told Lou to have the boys round up what gear they could and head back to their headquarters in Red Harlem. He'd help Nariaal look for Lieutenant Vohn and reunite with the gang sometime in the morning.

Nariaal padded on large, hand-like feet down the corridors, now empty save for the occasional corpse or scattered gear. Jimmy followed with both hands gripping the looted ray carbine, but no resistance was encountered.

They found Sinari in the burned-out crystal lab, standing over the crumpled, dead body of Dr. Rotwald. Her face was a strange mask of confusion, elation, and bitterness. Zed stood frozen in place, not turning to face them when they entered. Remarkably, the walls and ceiling of the hollow chamber were still intact, though charred as if by some colossal explosion.

"We appear to have taken the facility, Lieutenant," Nariaal greeted.

Sinari said nothing for several moments, staring down at the corpse of her quarry.

Finally, it dawned on her how large he'd loomed in her own head. She had made him into a Goliath, when in fact he was just a man. Mars had its own tradition of autocrats, and what Terrans called "fascism". This was nothing new. But in the end, those warlords with their portraits and their statues and their brutality were just men. And they bled and died as easily as any other man. They were often replaced with another brutal dictator, another despot. But sometimes, society replaced them with something better. More humane. More just.

Dr. Rotwald, scientist and face of the Third Reich on Mars, was no more. There were still a handful of mining outposts elsewhere in the remote desert, but the Nazi plot to flood the crystal market with defective thermacite was over... for now.

The first mission of Lieutenant Sinari Vohn's unit of Space Rangers was complete.

Sinari took a slow breath, finally taking notice of the ape. "Zed took a hit, looks like he shut down. Can you check him out?"

Nariaal nodded, turning his attention to the robot as Jimmy approached the center of the room.

"Is that Rotwald?" he asked, pointing his weapon at the body lying face-down at Sinari's feet.

"It is."

Jimmy regarded her with a raised eyebrow. "So, Lieutenant. Looks like you're done here."

"Looks like."

"Does that mean you're cutting me loose?"

"It does."

Jimmy relaxed visibly with the news, but Sinari had a few details to reiterate.

"Remember, Jimmy. No running defective munitions, and no trafficking in *people*. This amnesty is limited. Stick to petty crime and you'll stay under my radar." She glanced around the vast room. "Who knows? Maybe consider going legit. This place would make a good lounge and casino."

That caught Jimmy's attention, and she could see the wheels in his mind begin to turn.

"Casino..." he muttered, thoughtfully stroking the thin patch of hair on his chin.

Sinari smiled. "AEGIS would probably let you have the lease for next to nothing... once I file my report and recommendations."

Jimmy stared at her in near disbelief. "You'd do that?"

"You scratched my back, Jamar the Gold. It would be dishonorable not to scratch yours."

"I need to take Zed back to the workshop," Nariaal announced. "I can't do the necessary repairs here."

Sinari nodded her head toward the exit. "Shall we?"

"You know," Jimmy paused, putting his cart miles ahead of the horse, "you could always come work for me. You're good under pressure and you fight like a demon. You'd make a lot more money..."

Sinari rolled her eyes and pointed at the door. "Don't press your luck, Jimmy."

The Venusian gangster shrugged, slinging the carbine to his shoulder. "Just a thought."

The trio made their way back to the vehicle bay with Jimmy in front, Nariaal carrying the rigid robot under one massive arm, and Sinari limping to keep up. A few Martians were in the process of collecting their dead for funerary rites, and stripping the dead SS troops of weapons and gear. Sinari decided to leave them to it—after all, this place had been a citadel for their people long ago. By all rights, it belonged to them. Not that the colonial powers saw it that way.

She caught the eye of a tribesman and bowed her head in solemn respect, offering up a brief prayer to the Goddess. The warrior returned the gesture, black hair and ruddy skin slick with sweat.

Early morning light bathed the canyon outside the loading dock in stripes of pink and gold. The Long Canyon tribe had arrived with their own vehicles for transport of their dead and any salvage they could lay their hands on. Word had spread about Lieutenant Sinari Vohn, and every warrior she encountered offered a reverent nod or bow.

Marshal Henry Hu was a bit late to the party, having mustered a small posse in Carter Flats to ride out to Long Canyon and help if they could. Still, they'd been able to apprehend a handful of SS troopers fleeing into the desert, so AEGIS would have some live prisoners to interrogate after all.

Sinari was shocked at his arrival in the vehicle bay, as he hadn't been privy to the assault plans. "Marshal Hu?"

"Need any help here, Vohn?"

"Um, no," she blinked. "How did you—?"

"Colonel Stevenson asked me to check on you," the Marshal grinned. "I owed him a favor, so here I am." He offered a quick wink. "Besides... I like you, Vohn. Looks like you took these Nazis to the woodshed."

"I guess so," she replied quietly, not knowing what the metaphor meant, and still not confident in the appearance of her success. "Will you keep some deputies posted here until we can send some AEGIS personnel back to take operational control?"

"Say no more, Vohn," he nodded, waving her away. "Get outta here."

Once everyone was safely aboard the grav sled, Drake shrugged out of the jump pack and moved to the pilot's chair, while Nariaal tended Sinari's punctured knee. Jimmy, miraculously, had acquired only a few scrapes and bruises. He maintained it was because he was so adept at combat, not due to his avoidance of it.

Sinari plopped down in one of the passenger seats and leaned forward, draping an arm across the back of Drake's chair as the sled zipped through the canyon. "You did good, Dawson."

Drake managed a tired smile, bandaged left arm shaky at the controls. "Thanks, Vohn."

Sinari stole a quick glance in the back at Tana, who was still loopy from being drugged. "Thank *you*," she offered in Drake's ear, "for getting my sniper back."

"*Our* sniper," Drake corrected. "We're a team. Of course we went back for her."

Sinari sat back and slouched in abject exhaustion. She pondered his words, smiling at how they felt in her mind. *We're a team. Of course we went back for her.*

"Of course we did," she muttered.

They dropped Drake where the new rocket fighter stood at the northern mouth of Long Canyon, and he departed their company to fly it home. Sinari took over the pilot's chair in the skiff, whisking her passengers back to the city in his wake.

When they arrived at AEGIS headquarters in Mars 1, the sun was already rising in the sky, twinkling off the gleaming glass and chrome geometry of the bustling spaceport. Tana went directly to the infirmary to sleep off the remainder of the narcotic, while everyone else got a cursory exam and retired to their respective quarters. Jimmy was released, and met on the spaceport steps by Lou and a maroon Packard sedan.

"Lou, me boy," Jimmy gave a broad grin, in spite of his fatigue. "What do you think about the casino business?"

"I *like* the casino business?" Lou raised a curious brow as he ushered Jimmy into the back seat and pulled the car into traffic.

Colonel Stevenson met Sinari in the hallway as she trudged to her quarters to sleep for a year—*so help me, a whole year if I could manage it.*

"Everyone back in one piece, more or less?" he quipped under the bushy mustache.

"More or less," she sighed.

"I look forward to reading your report," he said, clapping a firm hand on her shoulder. "After you get some rest."

"Yes sir." The acknowledgment was performative—she was barely coherent as it was.

Sinari made it to her tiny apartment and peeled off her jumpsuit. It was torn and shredded, plastered with dust, and reeking of smoke. There was a fresh one in her closet, but she wasn't donning the blue just yet. She stepped into the shower for a few minutes, rinsing away the last couple of days. Days which replayed in her head in flashes. From bringing in Creepy Karpis to her assignment heading up her Space Rangers unit, dinner and dancing with Ensign Dawson, and leveraging Jimmy Two-Fingers into the fight.

Closing the water valve and exiting the stall, she quickly toweled off, shedding the day's activities with the moisture on her skin. She wasn't sure which was worse: the fact that she'd had to kill so many Nazi soldiers, or how little remorse she felt about it.

She briefly considered the paradox of a free and tolerant society allowing for intolerant factions and ideologies to take root. But just as when a Martian warlord broke the social contract in ancient times and was cast out of society, she reckoned it should be the same with this new brand of fascism. A free society need only be intolerant of intolerance. And it should be swift and decisive in putting down despotic, authoritarian ideologies which break the social contract and threaten the lives and rights of free beings.

In that moment, Sinari knew she was of a much harsher and more radical worldview than she'd ever thought. She didn't feel remorse for killing those Nazi soldiers. In fact, she found herself steeled for the long haul of possible war, and almost looked forward to killing a few more.

Collapsing naked into her bed, she fell asleep immediately and dreamed of the giant flag again. The crimson banner with the black swastika in a white ellipse—and her pulling the thread that drew ever closer to the center. This time, however, the thread was on fire, crackling and searing as it unraveled the weave of the fabric, line by line. The fire grew larger and hotter with each line pulled loose, as it ignited the rest of the flag, engulfing it... eating away.

Until the fabric fragmented into fiery embers, consumed to nothingness.

CHAPTER 20

Sinari slept well into the day and emerged from her quarters with a clean uniform and equally fresh resolve. The corners of her lips approximated a sly smile. She'd had her first win. Terran sports enthusiasts would phrase it as being "one and O". Of course, as the analogous sports season wore on, her potential to rack up numbers in the losses column would loom larger. But that meant it was all the more important to revel in those wins. To savor them. She found it gave her outlook a renewed sense of duty, and her stride an extra bit of swagger.

Entering the science lab, she found Dr. Nariaal tinkering with some sort of gear box that was tilted outward from the back of Zed's chest cavity. The robot's eye was aglow in its usual blue-white hue.

"Doctor. Zed."

Nariaal glanced up from his work to regard her through his protective goggles. "Ah, good afternoon, Lieutenant."

Zed tilted his giant eye. "I would get up, but the good doctor is repairing some damage to my internal motor."

"I'm just glad to see you back up and running." Sinari exhaled a relieved sigh.

Zed added a curious angle to his head's position. "As previously stated, I cannot currently 'run', as my motor functions—"

"Relax," Sinari offered. "It's just an expression."

Nariaal nodded at the gauze wrapped around her knee. "How's the leg?"

Sinari winced almost automatically at the reminder. "It'll take some time to heal, I suppose, but if I sit still it'll just lock up."

"Indeed," he nodded, indicating the bandage around her arm. "And the burn?"

"It's a burn," she shrugged. "Would've been a lot worse without you both. You really pulled this thing through, and I just wanted to say thanks."

"You're most welcome, Lieutenant," Nariaal said as he returned to his work.

Sinari realized how understated her thanks had been compared to the actual deeds performed, but she also thought it best not to belabor the point. Everyone needed time to recover and process what they'd been through.

She left Nariaal to his work and bumped into Drake as he was exiting the medical bay. He too wore a fresh blue jumpsuit.

"How's Tana?" Sinari asked.

"Resting," Ensign Dawson said, brushing a calloused hand over a recently shaved jawline. "Doc gave her some fluids. The drugs should be out of her system in another hour or so." He paused, watching her face relax. "How are you?"

Sinari blinked, finding an efficient smile in her emotional costume trunk. "Nothing a good night's sleep or ten can't fix. Got some new scars from that burning thermacite. Should make for a good bar story."

Drake found himself blushing for some reason. "We all need a good bar story."

Before she knew what was happening, before she could listen to the responsible adult in her mind, she coiled around him like a serpent, kissing him firmly, passionately. She pressed him to the wall, tongue probing his mouth—and finding his reciprocating. He smelled of laundry starch and Burma-Shave, and a hint of human pheromone that made her lightheaded. His hands found her waist as she held his face and neck in her embrace. The act was intense, lasting only a few seconds, though it felt far longer.

What are you doing? she thought, finally taking a moment to collect her wits and relax her grip on Dawson. Righting herself and adjusting the sleeves on her uniform, Sinari cleared her throat. "I, uh... I'm..." she sputtered. "Apologies, Ensign."

Drake took a lengthy breath as reality set in. Kissing a fellow officer was not something encouraged—or in point of fact allowed—by active duty AEGIS field agents in uniform. But it wasn't unwelcome. And it was probably to be expected somewhat, from two comrades bonded together through crisis. "No apologies necessary, Lieutenant."

His gleaming, roguish smile told her everything.

"I need to check in with Colonel Stevenson," she said, taking a step back to a professional distance.

Drake nodded in agreement. "I need to write up my report," he said rubbing the back of his neck. "But I was gonna go into Red Harlem later, maybe look for a card game..." he trailed off, then stepped into the space

Sinari had put between them. "If you'd care to join me."

Sinari had the advantage of her copper Martian complexion to hide her flushed excitement. "I would enjoy that, Ensign."

"Outstanding, Lieutenant," Drake winked pulling away down the corridor. "1800 hours?"

"1800," she repeated. "Meet you on the front steps."

"Drinks?" Drake asked, already several paces away. "Cat's Meow?"

Sinari chuckled. "Absolutely."

As she turned to head in the opposite direction, she failed to notice Tana sitting upright in her hospital bed, watching the scene in the hallway through the open infirmary door.

☙

"Come in, Lieutenant... Commander," Colonel Stevenson smiled from his desk, beckoning Sinari into the dimly lit office. "I pushed the paperwork through this morning."

Initially shocked at the news of her promotion, she entered with a stride that was full of the confidence the past few days of punishing Nazis had given her. "Sir? Are you sure—?"

"AEGIS has a mandate out here, Vohn." Stevenson rose from his chair and ambled to the corner of the desk, a similar swagger in his step. "The fight against fascism is heating up, and the Space Rangers are our ace in the hole. That means we need to promote candidates who show the most promise, despite lack of resources. You proved yourself to be one of those individuals when you completed the mission."

Confidence. That's what it was. The experience of doing the impossible and coming out alive—albeit with the scars to prove it had been real. Stevenson's adventures were from an earlier era, fighting occult fascists on Earth. But the experience informed who he was, and continued to serve him in this next stage of life and career.

"Lack of resources should not be an issue in the future," he added.

Sinari stood in the formal "at ease" position, legs slightly apart, arms behind her back. "Sir, I haven't even submitted my report."

"And I look forward to reading it. Nariaal debriefed the moment they got back, so I got the gist. I also got a brief rundown from Marshal Hu." Stevenson displayed a half-grin which broke the left side of his face into a maze of fine lines and wrinkles. "Bottom line:

you gave the Nazis a bloody nose. They're already scrambling to fill the void left by Rotwald's demise." He met her gaze with an unexpectedly intense look. "Just tell me it was painful."

Momentarily stunned by the apparent bloodlust in her commanding officer's question, Sinari realized he'd been behind a desk long enough that he was living vicariously through his younger subordinates. She cracked a mischievous smile. "Very painful," she answered quietly.

"Good," Stevenson nodded, returning to a more businesslike posture. "Any commendations you wish to submit along with the report?"

"Ensign Dawson," she blurted, a bit too earnestly. "Ensign Tana. Doctor Nariaal. And Zed."

Stevenson's eyebrow arched curiously. "The robot?" He could see her flinch slightly at the word.

"The robot saved my life, sir. I would like it to be a permanent resource for my unit."

"I see. And what about your... criminal asset, Jimmy Two-Fingers?"

"In exchange for his assistance with this mission, and on his commitment to cease all humanoid trafficking, I promised to expunge his record on Mars."

Stevenson pursed his lips in thought. "Anything else?"

"I offered him the use of the Long Canyon laboratory site as a casino." She winced as she said it aloud. It seemed like such a good idea when she'd made Jimmy the offer, but now she wasn't so sure. Even so, she needed to try to salvage the plan. "I figured it would offer employment for local Martians outside the mining industry, and better serve us to keep his activities within our sights... sir."

Stevenson's eyebrow lifted again. "Excellent idea, Vohn. Strategic thinking."

Sinari exhaled, relieved. She produced her printed report from behind her back and handed it to Stevenson. "Will there be anything else, Colonel?"

"In the near term? No. Take a week off for some R&R. Go have fun." He wandered back behind his desk, placing her report on the blotter. "I know you're aware of the fraternization rules within AEGIS field service..."

"I am, sir."

Stevenson smiled warmly. "But if I don't know about it, and it doesn't become a morale issue..." He trailed off, punctuating the remark with a shrug and a wink.

"And the long term, sir?"

Stevenson paused, glancing away briefly before returning his attention to her. "Our latest intel reports that a Nazi SS officer named Bruno Müller has been given command of a new paramilitary unit called the *Raumwaffen.*"

"Raumwaffen?" Sinari mused. "That means... *space weapons* in German."

"Correct," Stevenson sighed. "Müller's already got a foothold on the Lunar surface, and an operation on Venus. I assume he'll be moving troops to Mars, to shore up their thermacite mining interests, now that Rotwald is out of the picture." He sat in the chair behind the desk with a slight grunt of resignation. "So in the long term, things are going to get really hot in the cold of space."

"I see." Sinari lowered her head in simple frustration. She'd witnessed the rapid rise and fall of despot warlords on Mars prior to Terran occupation. *Must it always be this way? One power-hungry madman replacing another until the root cancer is cut out?* Realizing she'd answered her own question, she pulled herself together, adopting the confident stance once more. At the very least, she'd make a good exit. "Thank you, sir."

Colonel Stevenson fixed her with a warm look. "Seems like such a daunting and never-ending task, doesn't it? But you did good, Vohn. Better than good. We licked the Central

Powers in the Great War, and we licked the *Astrum Argentum* after that. And we'll lick these Nazis and send them packing as well. But it'll take time, and effort, and as much grit as we can muster. And you've demonstrated you've got it—in a seemingly inexhaustible supply." He turned his attention to the report on his desk and waved her toward the office door. "Now go on. Dismissed. Go have some fun. I don't want to see you for a whole week."

Sinari noted his smile as he gestured at the corridor. She matched it as she nodded her acknowledgment. "Sir."

Turning on her heel, she exited the office and disappeared down the hallway.

ᘓ

Sinari and Drake met on the front steps of the spaceport, just as they had earlier in the week. But this time the chemistry between them was far more pronounced, and neither bothered to deny or ignore it. Without the constraints of an active mission timeline, they were free to indulge. Drinks at the Cat's Meow, with their house jazz band, followed by dinner and dancing at the Canyon Club, and a poker game at a quaint joint called Ray's.

As the evening wore on, word began to spread that a couple of AEGIS Space Rangers who'd shut down the Nazi crystal operation were enjoying a night out in Red Harlem, and local Martians began to seek them out for a handshake or to buy them a drink. After the first round or two, neither Drake nor Sinari had to seek their respective pocketbooks for cash. If it wasn't local Martians paying, it was the club management comping them.

One or more of the strangers buying rounds might have been spies. But Sinari decided at the moment she didn't much care.

All Nazi spies will get a fist in the face or a raygun blast to the chest, eventually. Queue forms on the left.

They ended up in a hotel suite in the heart of the neighborhood—also comped. There they coupled into the early morning, despite bruises and burns, bandages and sore ribs. With the sexual tension finally broken, the pressure relieved, they would be able to take a breath and proceed at a leisurely pace from then on.

The flickering neon lights of Red Harlem painted the hotel room walls in vibrant, shifting patterns as they nestled together in carnal afterglow, finally drifting off into unconsciousness.

After three hours of heavy, death-like sleep, Drake awoke to find a note on Sinari's pillow. It simply said:

Had a great night. Heading to Carter Flats for the day.

Dinner later?

XO,

Sinari

Drake smiled, watching the sun rise high in the Martian sky.

Sinari took her Triumph out of the garage and sped across the desert to Carter Flats for a visit with Marshal Hu, giving him all the raucous details of the mission, comparing notes, and showing off her wounds. Henry just grinned and nodded along with the tale, gleeful to see her so animated. And it wasn't just the mission. She was lighter somehow, a bit less guarded.

Maybe in love? he thought.

Yes. Yes, definitely in love.

With Sinari's mission commendations came promotions for Drake Dawson and Tana to the rank of lieutenant. Nariaal, already a major, declined promotion in lieu of a larger laboratory budget, and the robot Zed was added to the personnel roster as a full-time squad member.

Tana became noticeably quiet following her release from the infirmary, keeping her teammates—Dawson especially—at arm's length. Although everything appeared "strictly business" from the outside, Drake Dawson assumed her somewhat frosty demeanor was due to having witnessed a certain kiss between certain fellow officers in a certain hallway. It puzzled him greatly. After all, it was Tana who'd ended their brief affair prior to both of them being picked for the Space Rangers unit. As far as he was aware, any romantic ship they'd sailed prior to this mission had left port without them.

Ultimately, he reckoned maybe she'd had a change of heart as a response to the trauma of being drugged and rescued.

Or maybe Venusians were just chaos personified when it came to matters of the heart. He'd only met two, and one of those was Jimmy Two-Fingers, so his experience was limited.

Shortly thereafter, the AEGIS R-22 rocket fighter was added to the assets available to the Space Rangers, and Colonel Stevenson grabbed four of them for the Mars unit. Flight training began soon after they returned to duty.

Dawson was quick to customize his bird with the illustration of a pair of dice showing double ones and the name *Snake Eyes* painted on the wings. Following Drake's example, Tana named hers *Flyin' Tiger*, adding the caricature of a Venusian feline's snarling face. Sinari decided to follow suit with *Crimson Shark,* and a cartoon drawing of the Terran predator fish she'd learned about in her technical research.

Work on the Long Canyon Casino & Resort began almost immediately. After AEGIS security personnel swept the complex and removed the remaining bodies and any tech that hadn't been picked over by the local Martians or Jimmy's gang, contractors were brought in to make the necessary renovations.

With the most serious charges on his criminal record expunged, Jimmy Two-Fingers supervised every project personally, taking full advantage of the effective mulligan Sinari had given him. Lt. Commander Vohn popped by when she could, monitoring progress and keeping Jimmy on track.

Within a few short months, the place was transformed. A casino floor with game tables replaced the crystal laboratory. A lounge with a full performance-worthy stage and bandstand was added where the ancient throne room once stood, and a subterranean swimming pool was fed from the local aquifer. Roulette, craps, table games, and slot machines occupied their own floor, and the old soldier barracks from the tribal era were converted into hotel rooms and suites.

Excitement was building in Mars 1, Carter Flats, and the entire surrounding region. The Long Canyon Casino & Resort was likely to be a huge success, and a colossal money-maker for Jimmy's outfit. And a lot of native Red Martians would be employed in jobs that did not include breaking their backs in the thermacite mines.

Just three weeks prior to its grand opening, workers drilling to fit electrical conduit in one of the sub-levels stumbled on an ancient inscription carved into the rock above a corridor which had been sealed with Martian concrete eons ago.

The carving was simple, but to the point:

TOMB OF ELDERS – DO NOT ENTER

The End

The Space Rangers will return in

Prisoners of Venus

ABOUT THE AUTHOR

Todd Downing's love affair with genre storytelling dates back to his consumption of classic radio dramas and comic books as a child in the 1970s, which broadened into a general appreciation for sci-fi and fantasy media of all kinds.

He grew up in the greater San Francisco Bay Area, writing and drawing from a young age, his works ever-present in school literary journals and newspapers, and eventually on film. He married his high school sweetheart and moved to Seattle in 1991 where he began to write professionally, and worked as an artist in the videogame industry until his publishing company became a full-time operation, while raising two children amid the chaos.

Downing is the primary author and designer of over fifty roleplaying titles, including *Arrowflight*, *Grimmworld*, *Airship Daedalus*, and the official *Red Dwarf* RPG. He continues to write genre fiction for stage, film, comics, audio, and adventure gaming products.

Widowed to cancer in 2005, Downing remarried in 2009 and currently enjoys a mostly empty nest in Port Orchard, Washington, with his wife and a rotating roster of rescue cats. Fortunately, he has an office with a door that closes.

OTHER WORKS

Calico Kids

Return of the Calico Kids

The Parish

Sakuru

Primordial Soup Kitchen
A Collection of Short Strangeness

Airship Daedalus series:

Book 1: *A Shield Against the Darkness*

Book 2: *Assassins of the Lost Kingdom*
(by E.J. Blaine)

Book 3: *The Golden City*

Book 4: *Legend of the Savage Isle*

Book 5: *The Arctic Menace*

Book 6: *Raiders of the Red Storm*

Plus:

AEGIS Tales
A Retro-Pulp Anthology, Volumes 1 & 2

AVAILABLE NOW
in ebook and print!

Join the author's mailing list:
www.todddowning.com

www.ingramcontent.com/pod-product-compliance
Lightning Source LLC
Chambersburg PA
CBHW031524310726
48971CB00008B/2344